DEMON HEART

CURSED HEARTS, BOOK 2

RHYS LAWLESS

RHYS WRITES Romance

Demon Heart, Cursed Hearts Book 2

Copyright © 2019 by Rhys Lawless

Cover Design by Ethereal Designs

Editing by Victoria Milne

Proofreading by Alphabitz Editing

 Created with Vellum

ONE

CALEB

The phone buzzed for the hundredth time that day, and once again, I ended the call before it rang.

Graham could wait. I didn't want to talk to him. Preferably, I'd rather not talk to him ever again. After everything we had discovered about the high council, there was no way I was associating myself with them again. Which was a shame, really. Before all hell broke loose last week, I'd had aspirations of becoming a member myself one day.

But after everything we'd discovered, after everything that had happened and all the terrible indescribable things the high council had done, the likelihood of my becoming a member was low. And that's how I wanted it to be anyway.

I should have learned my lesson by now. I had gone through enough shit in my life to still believe that everything was as it seemed. The army hadn't been what I expected. Then the vampire world was different than they made it out to be. Even life as a human was far less fascinating than the movies and books presented it. I'd seen the best and the worst in people time and time again. I should have seen this whole ordeal coming.

And no, I wasn't being overdramatic. Anyone who discovered their governing body that everyone put so much trust in had consented to murdering innocent people would have had the same reaction.

Not that it made a difference, but they hadn't just consented to the murdering of innocent people, but the execution of people they'd been sworn to protect. Fellow witches. And to make matters even worse, they'd been giving up the lives of innocent, new, fledgling witches who had no idea what the fuck was going on. It could have happened to anyone. It could have happened to me if I hadn't been involved in that shit involuntarily.

While I didn't want to associate myself with them, I couldn't abandon my post at Java Jinx, the cafe Lorelai and I had been running for some years now. Partly because I would have to find a new career, and at my age, and with my circumstances, that would be hard enough, but also because I needed to find a way to protect the witches that didn't know the truth, which was the vast majority of them. I didn't want to create an uprising because that would only lead to more disaster, but there had to be a way to knock the high council off their high horses and replace them with people who actually deserved to be there.

"Will you tell me why you're not talking to Graham? What did he do to you?" Lorelai asked.

No, I hadn't had the guts to tell her yet. Lorelai had grown up among witches and was close to many. I didn't know if I had the balls to tell her what the coven she'd grown up in had done and tear apart her faith in everything. I'd been through that shit, and she didn't deserve it.

"It's nothing you need to be concerned with. This is just between him and me."

It hurt lying to her. Thank goodness her sense of smell couldn't detect lies because I didn't feel like I was doing a good job as it was.

"One day I'll get it out of you, you know that?" she said.

And one day I would tell her. When I had a solid plan of how to bring those monsters down.

"How is little Nora?" she asked. "And please tell me *he* died in a fire or a car accident since I last spoke to you."

And by *he*, she meant Wade. My witch hunter boyfriend. It had been one hell of a week, so a witch hunter being my boyfriend was the sanest statement to come out of the shit show last week. Somehow, we'd managed to avoid the news spreading about our relationship, but I didn't know how long that would last, not that I cared much about other witches' opinions.

Graham might be looking for my forgiveness, but he also didn't like the fact that I was seeing a guy he considered dangerous. It was in Graham's best interest to keep it secret as long as possible anyway. He owed me for what he'd put me through.

"Lorelai! Behave, please," I said.

She threw her hands in the air in a surrender only an idiot would believe.

"Fine. I will not speak ill of the dead...ly man in your life. Are you still letting him loose around Nora?"

I raised an eyebrow at her, and she gave me one of those looks that said she had no idea what I was getting upset about.

"I am. And he thinks he has to do more than he does for her. Just because he promised Nora he'd help me take care of her doesn't mean I need him to be her father. It's too soon for this kind of shit anyway. This last week, his entire world has changed. He found out he had been manipulated his entire life and he'd been feeding a dhampir instead of doing the angels' work. The last thing he wants is for me to burden him with a baby. Annabel and I have done it for six years, and we can do it for as long as needed."

Okay, that was a lie. While I loved Nora, and Annabel was one of my closest friends, the thought that I had to do another six years of looking after Nora, plus the twelve until she became an adult, was making me quite agitated, and I was annoyed with myself for feeling that way. Nora, my immortal phoenix, friend-adopted daughter, had saved mine and Wade's lives from certain death. She'd sacrificed herself for me twice. The least I could do for her was look after her.

But was I being selfish if I wanted to be just a normal adult for a while? I'd made no choices in my life. Fate had taken them all from me. It was fate that had decided I had to be a vampire and that I had to lose the people I loved over and over again.

It was fate that had decided to bring me to Nora and to have her introduce me to this strange world of Nightcrawlers and witches I never knew existed. It was fate's decision to bring me to the brink of death and have Nora sacrifice herself to give me my life back.

All my choices had been stolen from me. I'd had to roll with the punches that life was throwing at me, and I was getting sick of it. Because not only was I not living the life I wanted, but I also continued to live with the fear of losing those that I loved.

And it was true that I'd fallen in love with a witch hunter. I wasn't afraid to admit it to myself. I'd been denied him for years. Now that I had him back, I couldn't ignore our shared past, whether he remembered it or not. In one way, remembering our first time together gave me the permission I needed to feel something stronger for him.

I felt so many things for him I didn't even know where to begin. And he, despite the fact he'd chosen to not get his memories back, felt so much for me too. And he was acclimatizing to gay sex rather well. Yet I still had the fear at the back of my mind that I'd lose him. Like I'd lost everyone else before him. Either fate would work its magic again and split us apart, or he'd get himself killed by getting mixed up in my world. Because that's what happened to the people I loved. Granted, a guy leaving me was a far better fate than dying, but that was what it always came down to. One of only two options.

"Earth to Caleb." Lorelai clicked her fingers in front of my face, and I concentrated on her again. "Stop dreaming about gay sex with your new boy toy."

"He's not my—"

"Yeah, yeah, whatever you say, my friend. So, your little scum wants to be Nora's dad too? What will she call him? Insta-daddy?" She laughed, and I retaliated by glaring at her with evil eyes.

"Very funny," I snapped back at her.

Not that it wasn't true. And to be honest, it was a bit funny, but I'd worry about it when we crossed that bridge. Given my track record, Wade would be out of my life within the year.

A man walked through the door of the shop, and we both turned to look at Graham who wore his signature jeans and tucked-in T-shirt, his well-groomed beard hiding much of his face.

I got up to leave Lorelai with him, but he addressed me before I could escape.

"I came to see you, Caleb. It's important."

"I don't have anything to say to you. You can talk to Lorelai. I've heard enough of your bullshit."

Lorelai crossed her hands in front of her chest and stared at both of us, decidedly staying out of our conversation but trying to figure out what was going on. It was a wise decision.

"I know you're still mad at me, but we've got bigger fish to fry, Caleb, and I need your help," he said.

This man was unbelievable. Did he actually think that the small issue of them sacrificing young witches to a dhampir was not an important enough issue? Graham had once been the father I'd never had. He'd been there for me every step of the way, showing me how to be a witch and how to use spells, and lately, even how to make them. Even if it was just theory, he'd been teaching me. It had been a big step, preparing me to be his replacement. But after everything that had just happened, I couldn't look at him in the eye anymore. Because all I saw in those eyes was death and sacrifice.

"What could be a bigger fish than murder, Graham?" I said, purposefully being vague.

"I understand what we did was wrong, but it's not like your boyfriend is any better," Graham said, and he really shouldn't have done that. He had no right to talk about Wade.

"Wade has been controlled his entire life. He didn't have a choice in the matter. He was lied to over and over, and when he wasn't, he was ordered to do things he didn't want to. The high council made those decisions fully aware of the consequences. Wade might have killed a lot of witches, but you are the ones who put them in his hands."

Lorelai cocked her head towards me, puzzled by what was just said.

"Wait. What happened? What do you mean the high council put them in his hands?" she asked.

I didn't want her to find out like this. Not right now. Not when every decision we made was critical to how we brought those assholes down. But I couldn't hide it from her. She was my best friend after all.

So, I told her what we'd found out. Every uttered word making me feel sick and dirty as if I'd been the one that committed the crimes. My stomach tightened into knots, and I could feel the bile burning my throat.

"What? When were you going to tell me this? What the fuck is wrong with you?" Her last question was addressed to Graham, who looked at her with a red face.

"Lorelai, we had to do something until we could figure out a way to stop Christian. We couldn't let him go after every single one of us. We're not proud of it, or at least I am not, but we sacrificed the few to save the many, Nightcrawlers included."

Lorelai winced. She had obviously not liked what she'd heard. And she made sure to tell him.

"Is that how you justify murder? Killing the few to

save the many? That makes it right in your eyes? And you"—she turned to me—"I can't believe you didn't tell me. This is important. This affects familiars as much as it does witches. Were you going to let me work for a murderer for the rest of my life?"

"Lorelai, I wanted to tell you. I just didn't know how." I tried to explain, but there was no explanation. I'd been an idiot to keep it from her.

"I need some time on my own," she said and brushed her red hair up into a ponytail, which meant only one thing. She was going out in her fox form to think.

"I need to...go. I can't look at either of you right now," she said and ran out of the door, not even bothering to check if there were any people around before she turned into her animal form: a giant fox who dashed down the street away from us.

I turned to Graham and let my anger take over.

"See what you've done now? Why are you still here?"

"To talk to *you*, Caleb. It's about that night."

He didn't need to elaborate. There was only one night he could be referring to. The night Christian had killed me. The night he'd tried to tap into the ley lines and feed on the magic running wild underneath London. The night that had cost me my daughter.

"What about that night?" I asked him.

"You must've felt it too. The next day?"

"And?"

"Things have been happening since that night. Things we can't explain."

"I'm not working for the high council again," I said before he could go on.

"I'm not asking you to. But you need to help us understand what's happening. You were there that night. Maybe you can understand the mess."

"Figure it out yourselves," I said and tried to push him out of the shop. I was fully aware that this was his shop, that it didn't belong to me, but if they wanted me to run this business, it was mine until it wasn't.

"You don't understand, Caleb. People are dying. Something happened the night after. Something that ignited all the witches. Now there are hundreds of them running nuts in London, destroying themselves and others because they can't understand their powers."

That made me pause. Did he say hundreds of witches had been ignited? Igniting witches who didn't know who and what they were? That could only happen with a ritual, under controlled circumstances. Witches didn't just ignite. Their powers didn't just start manifesting.

"Why don't you just feed them to other creatures. I hear elves enjoy the occasional witch blood. I'm sure they'd enjoy the treat," I spat, still not willing to let this drop.

He looked at me with pleading eyes as if he hadn't committed murder. And if I wasn't so angry with him,

I'd forgive him and help him out. But as it was, I didn't wanna be in the same room with him any longer than necessary.

"Please, Caleb. The high council is willing to pay —" he started, but I squeezed his arm and pushed him towards the door.

"I don't want the high council's money ever again. Do you understand me? I'm running this business to help the witches you've betrayed. I'm not running this business to please the high council. Not anymore."

He froze, pleading still, despite everything I'd said. If I hadn't been wearing my gloves, as an empath, I would have felt everything he was feeling at that moment, but I didn't want to feel anything about him. I pushed him to the door and noticed the queue of witches outside the shop looking in through the glass.

And that was the moment it hit me. Lorelai had left me to run the store on my own at peak time on Friday. It had been hectic like this for a week now, since the day after Christian had almost killed us all. It was as if all the witches had felt the energy blasts that had woken both Wade and me. And if there was one thing that made money, it was scared witches looking to protect themselves.

"Now pretend you're giving me a hug and walk out of here. Don't come back unless you're delivering something," I said, and he did as instructed. His fingers touched the back of my neck. I didn't know if he did it on purpose or if it was an accident, but I forced myself to keep his feelings shut. Regardless, I still felt the pinch of guilt in my chest.

I didn't care for it. He had done terrible things. He didn't deserve my forgiveness.

I unlocked the door, and Graham left without another word, and just as I was about to let the witches in and start trading, Wade appeared in front of the queue and approached me.

"What are you doing here?" I asked him and pulled him inside the shop and locked it back up. A wave of disapproval echoed across the street from all the witches that were waiting. I gestured five minutes with my hand before I turned to Wade.

"Why are you here? I told you to stay away. We have a way of knowing witch hunters. And I don't want the news spreading. Not yet anyway."

"Are you ashamed of me?" He smirked, and, as usual, my need to wipe that smirk off his face overpowered me.

"What did he want here anyway?" he asked, nodding his head towards the direction Graham had gone. He might not have had the best opinion of Graham, but Graham had told him the truth about his BLADE force.

"He just came to tell me that the high council needed me for a job. Needless to say, I said no."

Wade stepped closer and put his hands on my arms. I didn't want anyone finding out about him, especially not the gossiping witches that were hanging outside the store, but I also couldn't resist his warm embrace.

"What kind of job?" he asked as he took me in his big arms and stroked the bottom of my hair, and I told him.

"I thought you wanted to help the witches of the coven?" he said.

"I do."

"Then why are you refusing Graham. They don't know what's going on or how to control their powers. And if they're hurting people, don't you want to help the innocent ones?"

Of course I did. There was no question about that. But I didn't want to do it for the high council. If they hadn't committed all these crimes the last five years, none of this would have happened.

I realized too late that not only had I thought that, but I'd also spoken it aloud because Wade's hands returned to my arms and he forced me to look into his eyes. The dashing blue eyes I couldn't say no to.

"Then let's help them. But let's not do it for the high council or the witch hunters. Let's do it for them. Because they deserve it. They deserve to know who they are," he said.

"Hey, someone wrote new lines for you. Where did you find them?" I said, and he gave me a gentle punch on the shoulder.

"Don't mock me, all right. I just came to say hi and to let you know I'm going back to the force."

"Have you heard from Lloyd yet? How is the new director? Willing to listen?"

When he'd told me he wanted to go back to the BLADE force, I'd thought he wanted to betray everything we'd gone through. But instead of letting me flip out, he'd simply kissed me and let all his emotions and thoughts on the subject rush into me to let me know he didn't want to do any of that.

"Gotta start from somewhere. Gotta stop all this senseless killing, don't we?"

"Good luck," I said, and he leaned in for a kiss.

"Good luck to you too. Find out more information. Then we'll help," he whispered in my ear and left, unlocking the door and letting the flock of witches rush into the store.

Damn, I didn't even get a chance to admire his ass as he'd left. I only had a limited time to enjoy it before he realized what a mistake he was making being with me.

Two
WADE

"So let me get this straight. You have suspicions that the director of your division is...inhuman, and instead of reporting it to us, you decide to work with a witch?" the man in front of me said.

His name was Leith Carter, and he ran the Edinburgh BLADE division. He was bald and carried a beer belly to rival any other beer belly on the planet, but he held himself like a true witch hunter. His eyes were dark and full of arrogance that I didn't appreciate. We'd been grilled for days and still hadn't come to a proper resolution. I would have thought revealing the true nature of Christian to the force would have given me and my brother Winston the leverage that we wanted. After all, we had revealed one of the biggest, longest scams in the history of the force.

I didn't know if Carter had ever met Christian, though I assumed he had, but Christian had fooled everyone, not just the hunters under his rule. I would have thought revealing Christian's intentions, his lies, and everything he'd done during his service at the BLADE force would have been less of this and more of the drink and toast kind.

It's not that I expected a gold medal and a promotion, although those would have been nice. I didn't even know if I wanted those anymore. After everything I'd witnessed, I didn't know if I could go back to hunting down witches and killing them.

No, I was sure, actually. I didn't want to do that.

I looked at Winston, who was sitting next to me staring into Carter's eyes and not saying a word.

"You have to understand, sir," I said. "I thought the force had been compromised. I needed to have proof and to understand the depth of the scam. I didn't just—"

He didn't let me finish. It'd been exactly how this meeting had been going for the last hour or so.

"What you did was terrible," he said. "Blades don't work with witches. End of. Whether or not your director was a vampire, that's not what we do."

"But, sir, spending time with witches has given me a great insight into their world. And I don't believe they're evil. I do believe Christian was making us kill out of incessant hunger. But not all witches are—"

"Sacrilegious," he hissed. He looked as if I'd insulted his mother, his father, and his entire extended family.

I shouldn't have been surprised. After all, if someone had told me a couple of weeks ago that I'd be working with and dating a witch, I'd have laughed in their face. I'd have thought they were messing with me. But things had changed. And I didn't know if they could ever go back to what they were.

"But, sir, we can't continue killing senselessly. We need to change. Otherwise, we're not any better than what we think witches are."

Those words were met with stares from both sides of the room.

Carter's eyes burned me, as did Winston's. It was impossible to believe that only a week ago this had been Christian's office. The bookcase was still full to the brim with books about angels and witches, and the desk still looked like it'd come out of the 1900s. Which, knowing who Christian had been, now made sense. The only thing that had changed had been the doors. Since the incident with Christian and that night, it felt like the force had implemented a transparency policy. Giving the vampire privacy had allowed him the leverage for years to do as he'd pleased. I didn't know how a couple of glass panels made a difference if someone wanted to kill cruelly, but this was not my battle today. My battle was to ensure the force did what was right and stop committing murders in the name of God and his angels. Were angels even real anymore? I didn't know. After everything that had happened, I wouldn't have been surprised to find out they weren't. However, if they were, I'd have been shocked if they approved of the crimes we'd committed against witches.

"No, sir, not sacrilegious. Humane. Christian made us believe for years that he knew what was right and that he knew the word of the angels when, in reality, he had no fucking clue. We have to do what's right. Right now, we're no better than terrorists. Just because an individual is a witch doesn't make them a danger to humanity," I said.

I didn't know if it'd go anywhere. The guy had been on our case since he'd arrived two days ago and didn't show any signs of letting go soon.

"What's wrong with you, Rawthorne? You've been the best in the field since you joined the force. What on earth could have happened in a few days to make you feel sorry for those sons of bitches?" Carter growled.

He looked from Winston to me as if it wasn't already obvious.

"I met one."

"You met one," he repeated and nodded along as if I'd admitted to the worst crime in human history. "I've read your reports. You seem to have gotten really close to the witch. But you see, Rawthorne, the reason why we don't fraternize with witches is because they're liars. They can manipulate the truth and twist it to get what they want, and what they want is to destroy us. And you..." He turned to Winston, and so did I.

Winston looked at our replacement director but didn't say anything.

"And you?" he asked Winston.

"And me what, sir?"

"Why are you here? You're not under investigation."

It was true. Winston was not under investigation. He hadn't betrayed the force or worked with witches like I had. He'd just been under Christian's control, like me, and had bonded for life with a raven familiar, not that Carter knew that.

As much as Winston supported the decisions I'd made, and how could he not when they'd given us our freedom back, he still didn't want to make his potential relationship with a half-witch, half-raven public knowledge. And from what I'd known, it wasn't any of those descriptors that made him feel insecure. It was the male part of the equation that did.

"That may be the case, sir, but I feel the same way as Wade. If last week's events have shown me anything, it's that there's more than one side to a story, and I can't in good faith continue doing my job if it's destroying innocent lives."

I was proud of my little brother. He didn't need to do any of this. He'd always been the aloof, do-what-I'm-told kind of guy, and he never questioned anything.

But now, not only was he questioning, he was taking the right side of history. And how could he not?

After everything that had happened, he'd made a decision to remember everything the dhampir Christian had made us do, and he had to live with the consequences of his actions. Whether or not he'd any control over those actions was a different matter entirely. One that had been messing with his head.

Thinking of all the terrible things I must have done for years that Christian had made me forget was a beast I hadn't even begun to comprehend. Had he made me fall for Sarah just to take her away from me and destroy me? It was entirely possible after he'd erased everything Caleb and I had gone through the first time we'd met.

I took comfort in knowing that at least my addiction to spell dust wasn't real. I hadn't had a craving for a spell since Caleb had liberated me. But everything else? Everything else was a complete mindfuck I didn't have the strength to navigate.

"That's very disappointing to hear from you, Winston. I didn't expect that. Has your brother brainwashed you already?" Carter asked, pushing his chair back and standing up to pace the room.

"No!" Winston shouted. "No more brainwashing for me."

Carter paused for a moment and stared at Winston, his expression an unreadable stone-cold slab before he continued with his pacing.

"I understand what you've gone through is difficult." He looked at Winston and then me. "Both of you. I'm not discounting what the dhampir did to you, but you are Blades. Hunters. Witch hunters. Your duty is to serve and protect humans from their evil kind."

"I can't do that in good conscience after all the lies and deception, sir. I simply can't," Winston said, and Carter's pursed lips told me he didn't like his answer.

He came and stood behind his desk again, his fists supporting him over the surface, his knuckles red from the pressure of his upper body.

"In that case, I'm afraid you are both dismissed from the force," he said, and I couldn't help but feel like a punch in the gut had been handed to me.

It's not that it hadn't crossed my mind, and it wasn't as if I was willing to stick around if the entire structure and alma mater wasn't going to change, but it still felt like I'd failed. At what, I didn't know, but the failure messed with my insides nonetheless.

I'd been in the BLADE force since I was sixteen, training hard to become the best of the best. After Mom's passing, it had been the only thing I could think of doing to take revenge on the witches I'd thought had cursed us and to find the one that had placed it on us. Being a hunter had been my entire life's purpose. Until I met Caleb. Again.

Then, everything had changed.

Not only did I find out we'd been lied to, but we'd also had memories stolen from us, fabricated, and replaced with different ones. And I'd found out the truth before. I had been made to forget that time, but this time, no one could make me forget. And if the force wasn't willing to change and do something about the slaughtering and senseless murder of witches, then I didn't want to be part of it anyway.

It'd just mean I'd have to work extra hard to protect the witches that the force went after, which had already dropped considerably now that the high council had stopped feeding them names of fledgling witches like they had done for Christian.

"Fine," I said and stood, turning on my heel ready to leave.

"Great. Glad we're in agreement," Winston added and also stood.

Before we got to the door, however, Carter spoke again.

"Make sure you leave your swords with Bruner."

It shouldn't have surprised me that we were being asked to submit our swords, but it did nonetheless. My blade had been mine since the very beginning. It was like an extension of my arm at this point.

It was infused with blood magic, however, and it had fed Christian for far too many years. I'd taken countless lives in the name of that egotistical, perverted monster. That sword had served its purpose, regardless of how twisted it'd been.

So why was I finding the idea of parting with it so hard? I should have ditched it the moment I'd found out the truth, yet I'd kept it. I hadn't used it, so at least I wasn't that bad, was I?

"With pleasure," Winston said and flung the door open, storming out.

I turned to give Carter a last look as if to say goodbye to this office and my career and everything that had happened to me through it.

Then, with a nod, I left too. It was time for a new chapter in my life.

THREE

CALEB

2 Weeks Later

I didn't know how many times I had to kick Graham out of the cafe for him to get the message, but I was starting to lose my patience with him and the people he worked for.

I'd agreed to keep moving his spells, not for him or the high council, but for the witches that needed protection. So I'd been okay with the deliveries he "had to monitor." Even if his presence was unnecessary, I'd allowed that—with boundaries, of course.

What I didn't tolerate was any more of this "you need to help us" bullshit that he was so well versed at. Sometimes I wondered if it was habit that made him come to me for help or if it was truly the high council asking for my aid.

"One of these days, I'm going to punch him so

hard, he's going to go through the wall and not stop until he hits Chechnya," Lorelai said as soon as we'd kicked him out.

At least I had her on my side again. I'd managed to explain what'd happened and had promised to keep her in the loop. After all, I hadn't been the one to murder innocent people for the sake of a bloody dhampir, so my forgiveness came easily.

She still couldn't see how or why I would ever want to be with Wade, and she made sure to mention it every day.

"So, has your scumbag boyfriend found a job yet?" she asked when we sat down with a cup of coffee.

It was a slow day at work and all the cleaning had been done as if by magic, so we could afford a few moments of normalcy, if you could call it that.

"He's not a scumbag, and no, he hasn't. Can you blame him? All he's ever done is kill people. It's not exactly interview material."

"Kill witches, you mean."

I'd hoped she wouldn't take notice of my word usage, but of course she had. Even though she was a familiar, she saw me and the witch community as family. Being orphaned from a very young age had been hard for her and finding her place in the world had been a challenge.

I knew that from experience. But unlike me, she'd had the support of the coven who had shown her everything she needed to know about herself and more. She, like me, had lost her faith in the high council after what she'd found out, but the rest of the coven had nothing to do with that bullshit, and Lorelai would stick to our side for as long as she breathed.

"I'm not having that argument again, El. It always ends up with spilled coffee and a broken mug, and you know how I feel about wasting good coffee. Also, don't get me started on our crockery budget. We simply can't afford to break any more shit."

She looked up, sighing and admitting defeat.

"Fine," she said. "What about the energy surges Graham wants you to look into?"

I winced.

"I'm not working for that asshole. I thought I was clear about that."

"I know, I know," she was quick to add. "But you can't tell me you're not curious to look into it. It's been three weeks since that night, and you've heard the horror stories."

The coven had been extremely busy trying to track the new witches down and help them tame their powers as well as teach them how to use them. And I'd be lying to Lorelai, and myself, if I said I didn't care.

I knew what it was like to feel helpless and desperate, not knowing where to turn or who to talk to and how to get answers to a million burning questions.

"I can't say I haven't been curious, but I don't want to work for them again, El. What they did was monstrous."

"Just because they did such an abominable thing doesn't mean those new witches who are scared and helpless need to suffer, does it?"

Before I could respond, the door opened, and Hew walked in wearing his leather jacket and a look of worry.

Saved by the raven. Thank the Goddess.

"Hey, what are you doing here?" I asked and Hew gave me a hug. Hew was a hugger, and as much as I hated hugging anyone other than Wade, one simply couldn't say no to Hew's cuddles or he'd sulk for days.

"I came to see you, of course, and to have one of Lorelai's fabulous pumpkin soya lattes."

Lorelai beamed at Hew's compliment, and she gave him a hug before she got started whipping up his coffee.

"What's up?" I asked and gestured for him to sit where Lorelai had previously occupied.

Hew took his leather jacket off, revealing his large, dark biceps underneath, and sat down. I wouldn't have thought a raven shifter would be buff considering how petite and light one had to be to fly, but here he was, buff nonetheless.

"I met with one of my brothers, and he told me you're investigating those ley line surges."

We'd hung out a lot since I'd got my memories back. The poor thing had been treated so badly by his raven brothers since he'd mated with Winston, it was heartbreaking. He'd already been the black sheep in the family considering he was only half-familiar, and bonding for life with a witch hunter had sealed the deal with his siblings. Not unlike me and the coven who had turned on me because I was with Wade.

"Where the hell did he hear that?" I asked.

Hew shrugged. "Chatter among the witches and familiars."

My fingers tightened into a fist, and Lorelai put down a cup of latte for Hew just in time before I spewed hate and vile.

"Fucking Graham is probably spreading the rumor to get me to do it. But no, I'm not looking into it, as much as the high council wants me to." I gritted my teeth.

"Why not?" Hew asked.

"Because he doesn't want to do anything for those assholes even if it'd be helping out witches that don't know how to use their power," Lorelai answered his question with the snark she was known for.

Great. All I needed was for two familiars to gang up on me.

"Oh, but Caleb, you have to. I can help you," Hew said. "This has been going on non-stop since that night. We need to find out what the hell is happening. If we caused—"

I raised my hand and Hew stopped talking.

"You didn't cause anything. If it was anyone's fault, it was probably mine. It was me Christian sacrificed to tap into the ley lines." I said the thing I'd feared to say aloud since the day after Christian's demise when that energy blast had woken both Wade and me.

Lorelai dragged a chair over from the next table and plunged herself on it to put her arms around me.

"Honey, is that why you don't want to look into this? It's not your fault. That douchebag was a manipulative piece of shit, you couldn't—"

"I couldn't have stopped him? Yes, I know. How do you think that makes me feel? I couldn't stop him from killing the high council members, and then I couldn't stop him from finishing his work. He might be dead, but the damage is done."

I'd gone through the events of that night over and over every day and night, and I'd tried to imagine what I could have done differently.

I could have not sacrificed myself to save Wade, but then he would have killed me anyway, or the witch Danielle would have finished me off, or Winston. It'd been an impossible situation, and I knew I'd done the only thing I could think of then, but now, I felt like shit about what had happened since. Whether or not I could have done things differently, it didn't matter. I'd still failed.

"Hey," Hew shouted and snapped his fingers in front of my eyes. "Don't do this to yourself, all right?"

"Do what?" I asked and refocused on him.

"Torment yourself about how you could have done things differently. There's no point, all right? Look at Winston. He chose to remember everything, but he didn't let all the things he did in the past dictate who he is. Instead, he's turning over a new leaf and trying to change the future, not linger on the past. And trust me, the things that monster made him do are atrocious." He took a sip of his pumpkin soya latte, letting out an orgasmic moan and winking at Lorelai. "This is magic, right here," he told her.

"I'd be lying if I said I didn't want to find out what's going on," I admitted while Lorelai and Hew stroked each other's egos, and they both turned to me.

"Excuse me?" Lorelai screeched. "I've been bugging you for two weeks to do something, and he convinces you within a second? I can't even begin to understand how I feel about this."

I gave her comment an eye roll.

"I didn't say I was convinced. I said it'd crossed my mind. There's a difference."

"Even so, you need to do something about it, and Hew can help you."

"I don't," I was quick to answer. "It's not my responsibility."

Hew reached out for my hand on the table and gave it a gentle squeeze. His index touched my bare wrist over my gloves, and his fear and compassion struck me to my core, and I had to pull back before they rendered me completely useless.

"Look at it this way," Hew said. "Would you rather the high council helps out those witches after everything they've done, or would you prefer it was someone they can genuinely trust and who can help them?"

He had a point. Who could guarantee the council didn't have an agenda still, and what would happen to those new witches whose powers they thought were useless? They might not have a dhampir to sacrifice them to, but who's to say they didn't have a dozen other catastrophic uses for them? After all, they'd committed an atrocity once, they could do it again.

"We'll see." Was all I managed to say. "I don't know if I have the energy to get involved in any of this crap again...but I'll think about it." Hew and Lorelai high-fived. "You guys are so immature."

Instead of taking offense, Lorelai pinched my cheek and gave me one of her silly grins.

"Whatever," I said. "Do you mind if I head? I promised Annabel I'd give her a break for a few hours, and I'd like to surprise her."

Lorelai looked around at the empty tables and huffed.

"It's going to be a struggle, but I think I'll manage."

"Thank you." I kissed her and ran to the office to grab my jacket.

"Say hi to both for me," she said before I left her alone with Hew.

Gods only knew what a mistake I was making leaving the two to scheme and plot.

———

As expected, Annabel had been more than ecstatic to have an afternoon off without Nora. After everything I'd put her through, I owed it to her. We'd worked through Nora's teething terrors together, and her terrible twos, threes, and fours, and we'd been more than happy when she'd finally started to settle and become somewhat a normal kid, and because of me, we had to go through this crap again.

I knew we weren't married, but I wouldn't blame her if she ditched my ass. Of course, that was assuming she didn't care for Nora. And Nora had been her best friend for a long time, so I knew she wasn't abandoning her any time soon.

There was a knock on the door and when I went to open it, I found Wade standing outside with that sinful grin on his face and a bag around his shoulders, and I had to stop myself from attacking him with my mouth in front of the entire high street.

Instead, I did the best next thing and grabbed his jacket, pulling him inside, and closed the door with my leg while my lips showed him how much I'd missed him.

"Can we do this every time I knock?" Wade asked, the grin now plastered on his face for good.

"Sure. I can't promise I'll always be this gentle, though," I told him, and in response, he spanked my ass, the slap audible even over my jeans. "Stop it.

Nora's upstairs, and she's awake, so don't get me riled up."

He pouted. Why did he have to pout when I was desperate to do things to him? I couldn't help myself. This man had been denied to me for years, and I'd only just found him again, both physically and mentally. I couldn't help myself for feeling crazy in love with him.

I made the pout disappear with another kiss and then, linking our hands, led him upstairs. When we entered the apartment, the first thing he did was walk over to Nora's crib and cooed at her.

"Has she slept?"

I laughed.

"Hah, does she ever? She seems hellbent on us not getting any sleep. Ever. I can't decide if she's doing it on purpose or not. Annabel says she wasn't like this when she was one before."

"Oh, no. Is Nora being a little nightmare?" he cooed and lifted her out of her crib.

I was going to stop him because I'd just made her calm down again, but for some reason, she was absolutely fine in Wade's arms. She didn't even wince. Instead, she actually started giggling when Wade made silly faces at her.

"See, I told you. She's doing it on purpose to get back at me," I said, my point proven.

"I think you're just being a drama queen," Wade replied, and I put my hands on my hips, which made him smirk.

I let my hands drop and pursed my lips.

"Hey, you don't get to call me that, newbie gay," I said. "You've only just learned the bloody word."

Wade turned Nora to face me and came closer.

"Nora, Daddy is being evil to me. We hate him now," he said and laughed at his own joke.

"You're not even her dad and you're making dad jokes now?" I crossed my hands in front of my chest.

Wade pierced me with his eyes.

"Evil!" he spelled out and pouted again.

No, not that pout. I fucking hated loving that pout.

"Okay, you're her surrogate dad, I guess. In a way."

Wade put Nora back in her crib and grabbed my hips.

"She made me promise to help you take care of her, so you can fuck off." He gave me a kiss and then let me go before I could do bad things to him.

I couldn't help myself in his presence. How could I? Those killer blue eyes and that naughty smirk did it for me every time, as did the sweet torment he put me through every time he touched me.

He put his messenger bag on the floor and sat down on the couch.

"Any luck with jobs?" I asked him.

Wade had been trying to replace the void left by the force for weeks now.

He'd tried security jobs, too, but considering he

couldn't exactly put down witch hunter on his resumé, it hadn't taken him far.

"What do you think?" he asked, and I joined him on the couch.

"Do you want me to help? I asked before, and I'll keep asking until you say yes," I said, only realizing too late how that had sounded.

Let's just hope he focused on my offer for help and not on how much that sounded like a proposal.

"It's fine. Really. I can do this. I don't need to get a job straight away anyway. I've got enough in savings to last a few months."

I knew he wanted to take control over his life after spending eighteen years under someone else's rule, but that didn't mean he couldn't take my offer of help.

"Okay. But you know I'm here for you, yeah?"

He nodded and leaned in for a kiss. His lips traced over mine, his breath raising the hairs at the back of my neck. I deepened our kiss and inserted my tongue into his mouth, and like a hungry monster, he pushed his tongue into mine to explore, making our teeth clash with the force.

My dick tightened in my jeans, and I desperately needed to let it loose. I put my hand over Wade's crotch, and I felt his hardened cock respond to my touch.

Don't do this to me, he begged.

"Why not?" I asked.

He opened his eyes and glanced at the crib.

"It's fine. We can go to my room," I said and picked up a spell from the table.

"What about Nora? We can't leave her on her own."

"We're not. She needs her nap, and this should help." I crushed the spell over her crib.

Indigo dust clouded over it and then a projection of the universe and its infinite stars swallowed up the room and took Nora's attention. She tried to grab a galaxy floating but then got distracted by the shooting stars.

"She'll be down in two minutes, tops," I said.

"That's handy," Wade said. "I'd still like to make sure, though."

I rolled my eyes. He was sweet, I gave him that, but when you'd been through this rollercoaster once, you knew the tricks to help you not go crazy. He'd never been a dad, and it showed.

"She's okay," I told him and tried to caress his cheek alluringly, but it didn't do anything to get his attention off Nora. "Serious boner killer. She's never going to go to sleep if you keep staring at her."

At that, he turned to look at me, and I nodded reassuringly.

"Trust me. She loves this projection. It's her own personal lullaby." I extended my hand to him.

His shoulders dropped and he grinned.

"If you're sure."

"Absolutely." I dragged him into my bedroom.

Once inside and with the door semi-closed, I threw him onto the bed and climbed on top of him, attacking his mouth in an effort to reawaken my boner and his.

It only took a literal slip of the tongue and a gentle touch on his abdomen, and we were both back where we'd left off.

He grasped my butt cheeks and squeezed over my jeans. I ground my crotch over his, and he panted in my mouth.

I want to fuck you, he said, and I responded by unbuttoning his trousers.

Let's, I replied and pulled everything off him so he was naked from the waist down.

I massaged his chest as I sat on his dick, grinding it against my jeans. He placed a hand back on my butt cheek and with the other hand, grabbed my jaw and urged me down to his mouth.

You're a tease, he said.

That's the point, baby. I let his tongue into my mouth again.

The hand grabbing my jaw moved down to my neck, and he squeezed, making my cock pulse in the confines of my underwear.

"Take it all off," he ordered with a sexy groan, and I obeyed.

I dismounted him and slowly unbuttoned my jeans, and then slid them off.

"Too slow," he said and pulled my T-shirt off, then

he yanked my underwear down to my ankles and pushed me head-first into the bed.

He opened my legs and before I knew it, I felt the moistness of his tongue tickle my rim.

You're killing me.

It's torture, isn't it, he said with way too much snark to go unnoticed.

His tongue pushed against my hole, and he moved his face up and down to lubricate me.

Fuck me already, I said, and he slapped my naked butt so hard a little yelp escaped.

Silence, witch. He spat on my hole and then used his tongue to spread the spit.

It'd been like this since we'd destroyed the crystal that had bound him to Christian, and I couldn't say I didn't enjoy it. Maybe a little too much considering we fucked every time we were together.

It was different than before. Five years ago, he hadn't been as kinky with me. I didn't know if it was because he'd been scared to let that side show, or because he hadn't discovered that aspect of himself yet, but now? He was unashamedly dominating me every time, just the way I liked, and he enjoyed our empathic connection way too much for his and my own good.

If death by orgasm was possible, I didn't think we had a lot of life left.

I felt something thick and hard prodding at my hole, and I let Wade's cock in me with a moan, which he silenced immediately by pressing my head on the mattress.

God, I hate you.

No, you don't.

You're right. I don't hate you. I love you, I said, and I felt him slowing down.

You— he started saying but was cut short when something hot scorched my back and I lost connection with Wade.

I turned over just as the magical dust settled over the bed and set it on fire.

"What the fuck?" Wade exclaimed.

I didn't have time to think it through. I burst the door wide open and reached for one of the crystals on the coffee table. I grabbed the sapphire blue and returned to the bedroom, flicking it over the bed.

"Extinguish," I shouted, and the blue sand sprinkled over the fire and the flames disappeared. My bed, or whatever was left of it, was covered in blue foam.

I looked at Wade, and he stared at me sheepishly.

"What did you do?" I asked him.

He shook his head.

"Nothing. One moment we were...you know, and the next I cough and this"—he pointed at the bed—"dust comes out of my mouth and sets the bed on fire."

I bent down and picked up my underwear to slip back on and then threw Wade's at him.

"You coughed magic dust?" I asked again.

"I think so."

"How is that poss—"

I didn't manage to finish my sentence because it dawned on me.

"Do you think it has anything to do with the spells you've used in the past?" I asked.

Wade raised his shoulders and shook his head.

"I don't know. Wouldn't the spells flush out of my system? I've been using for years." He put his trousers back on.

"Well, you never know with magic. But even if it's still in your system, you shouldn't be able to activate the spells. Only witches can. Unless..."

"Unless what?"

I walked out of the bedroom and into the living room, where Nora was fast asleep, and looked at the table of spells I'd been sorting out before Wade had arrived. It was a good thing I'd decided to do that, or we might have burned down the whole house. Lady Luck had definitely been on our side on this one.

Wade followed me and watched as I pulled an envelope from my bookcase.

I opened it and read some of the reports I'd collected from the newspapers and some Graham had dropped off, hoping to lure me into the case.

"Caleb, what's going on?" he whispered, glancing at Nora.

I closed the envelope and got close to him.

"I think the ley line surge is affecting you too. I

don't know why now, after all these weeks, but it seems the ley lines activated a spell you've consumed."

It didn't make sense, but if I'd learned one thing as a witch, it was that things rarely made sense when magic was involved.

"What?" Wade exclaimed and looked at Nora again. "It can't be."

I hugged him, but his body was rigid.

It's okay, I said, hoping to calm him down.

"It's not okay. What if it happens again?" he said and pulled away from me.

"It won't."

"How do you know that? What if it happens again when I'm holding Nora, or when I'm with you, or when I'm out in public? I nearly burned you alive. I couldn't live with myself if I hurt you or anyone else."

I grabbed his hands and gave them a squeeze, forcing him to look at me.

"We'll figure it out. Okay? I'll help you figure it out."

I guess I didn't have a choice in the matter anymore. I had to look into the case Graham, Lorelai, and Hew had been begging me to for weeks.

I had to if we were to make sense of what was happening to Wade.

Four
Wade

Why was this happening to me? Had I not been through enough? I'd had my childhood stolen and held ransom at the hands of an evil creature. I'd been made to forget I'd fallen in love once upon a time with a man and then had those memories replaced with those of an asshole partner that had got himself killed. I'd been made to kill Sarah and to think I was in love with her. I hoped the last part wasn't true, but I would never know the truth. Not with the crystal that had once controlled me destroyed. It was a small price to pay for not remembering everything else.

Wasn't all this enough? Did I have to suffer again? And not only suffer myself but make those around me suffer too?

It was the first time I'd had people who I cared about and who cared about me, and now I was putting them at risk with the stupid addiction Christian had given me to punish me for falling for the guy he was screwing.

And it wasn't just Caleb I could hurt if he was right in his assumption. It was Nora, Winston, Hew, Lorelai—who I knew didn't care much for me, but I liked her, and I didn't want anything bad to happen to her. Even Annabel, who hated my guts, could get hurt by this stupid thing, and I didn't want that.

I'd been a prisoner of that asshole for years, and now, when I'd finally thought I was free, this was happening to me.

Was it a life sentence? Had I pissed off the man above so much he didn't want to see me free or happy?

When I'd finally thought my life was starting to have meaning again and I was able to have access to all my emotions again, this fucking thing had to happen and put it all at risk.

I had to leave Caleb when Annabel returned home, and I felt guilty that he'd had to explain to her why his bed was scorched, but that didn't mean he'd stopped calling me.

He could help me. I knew that. But why should he have to?

Because he loved me?

Did he really mean it? How could he love someone like me? I was unlovable. Always had been. Cursed or not, I was a disaster. A murderer. A walking danger.

Turning a corner, I arrived on my street. I didn't

even know how I got there, but considering the bullshit going on inside my head, I wasn't surprised in the slightest.

I dug in my pocket in search of my keys and tapped the fob at the entrance to let myself in the apartment block.

I pressed the button to call the lift, and the doors slid open immediately. I hoped the incident was a one-off and it wouldn't happen again. Surely it couldn't happen again, right? It'd been three weeks without an incident, so surely this was a one-off.

Maybe the fire spell had been a delayed reaction from the last drag I'd had, and it had only come out of me by chance.

Yes, that was it.

I was panicking about nothing. It was all going to be all right. The incident at Caleb's house had been just that. An incident. It wasn't going to repeat.

Continuing to reassure myself, I pressed the button for my floor and waited for it to take me there.

I had to clear my mind, and I knew just the thing to do. Job hunting.

After two weeks, I knew why everyone hated it. There were way too many jobs, way too many scams, and way too much drilling to get anywhere. All I wanted was something to replace the BLADE force in my life. I didn't want anything fancy, although a job in security would probably suit me best considering what

I used to do for a living. But it was proving more than a challenge.

I had nothing to put on my resumé and couldn't find a way to explain what I'd done all my life. It wasn't easy explaining that I'd been manipulated my whole life into believing witches were evil and that I'd been hunting them down and killing them since the tender age of sixteen.

Gee, no wonder no one wanted to hire me. At least Winston was doing something with his life. Something to make up for what he'd done. He'd decided to set up a bodyguard service for witches and Nightcrawlers and help where needed. It was slow going, but the community was more trusting of him with a Raven for a mate. With Hew's help, he was doing some good anyway.

I would have loved to follow in his footsteps and do something similar, but I couldn't take the guilt I felt every time I thought of touching a sword again. It was bad enough interacting with Lorelai, who might not be a witch but felt like one. I couldn't even begin to imagine facing other witches after everything I'd done.

I was sure there was a way to atone for my sins, but I just had to find the thing that was right for me.

Of course, that assumed I could find something to do. Maybe I wasn't just unemployable, but also beyond saving.

No.

I refused to believe that just yet. I still had lots of

resumés to send, many things to try, and I would, goddammit. I wasn't going to give up that easily.

Something dry-choked me and I coughed, bending in half while doing so. Green dust sputtered out of my mouth, and before it reached the floor, it exploded.

Vines appeared out of nowhere and wrapped around every surface of the elevator and me.

No, not again. What the hell? Why was it happening again? This was supposed to have been a one-off. It wasn't meant to happen again. It couldn't be happening again.

I stretched my hands, trying to break free of the vines, but the more I did, the tighter they became.

This was my punishment, wasn't it? For killing all those witches and stealing their spells and allowing myself to fall for both Christian's and the force's lies.

Sure, I never had a chance to not believe anything Christian told me, but God didn't care about that, did he?

I pulled at the vine wrapped around my legs and felt the burn on the inside of my palms as the friction caused my skin to redden.

The one wrapped around my neck tightened dangerously and restricted the airflow. I felt like I was about to die in this bloody lift without having a chance to say goodbye to Caleb and Winston, and maybe even Annabel before I accepted the punishment for my sins.

My legs and fingers were going numb as my circulation stopped distributing evenly.

I wasn't going down that easily, dammit. I kept pulling and grabbing at every piece of the vine that I could. Surely there'd be a weakness in it. Somewhere. Anywhere.

Just as quick as the vines had appeared, they disappeared, leaving me alone in the lift to catch my breath and massage my bruised ego.

"What—" I started to say when the lift doors opened and Mrs. Weatherby greeted me in her usual manner with a cheeky grin and a wave of indifference.

She was wearing the same blue suit jacket and skirt as she always wore and the fascinator I was starting to think had been glued on her head because it was always appeared to be set on the same spot, every time I saw her. She stepped into the lift, and I nodded at her and leaned against the elevator's wall.

"Aren't you getting off, dear?"

How could she ask that when only moments ago I was fighting for my life? Because she hadn't been there to witness the horror. Thank goodness for that.

I was in serious need of help. What if this stupid spell had come out when I was with Mrs. Weatherby and it had killed her before I could stop it? Not that I knew how I'd stopped it, but that was beside the point.

Every step I took was putting someone in danger. I was a menace, and I couldn't ignore the signs anymore.

I had managed to put both Caleb's and my life at risk in under an hour. What could happen within twenty-four hours? What could happen within a week? I wouldn't always be lucky enough to have Caleb's help or to have the spell's strength expire, because I assumed that's what had happened.

I stepped out of the elevator and took another glance at Mrs. Weatherby, who smiled.

"Where is that lovely man of yours?" she asked.

"H-home," was all I managed to say before the doors closed and I was left to face my demons in solitude again.

I started to walk towards my apartment, but after a couple of steps, I couldn't bring myself to go any farther.

I had to get help, and I knew just the person to give it.

I turned on my heel and bounced down the stairs, running as if I was on fire. In one way, I guess, I was. The more time passed, the more danger I was putting everyone in. There was only one person I could think of who could help me.

Feeling slightly hopeful at the possibility of getting whatever was wrong with me fixed, I exited the apartment block that I'd entered moments ago and headed north. I would have taken the bus or train, but I was scared of what might happen if I did. Of what accidents I might cause. So instead, I walked. I walked all the way to Camden, flinching at every passerby and trying to keep my thoughts in check in case they had anything to do with the outbursts.

I didn't want to hurt anyone, even if they were strangers to me. My days of killing people were over and there was no return. There were no excuses anymore. I couldn't live my entire life blaming someone else for what was happening to me. It was about time to start taking charge of my own life, and as long as these spells were inside me, waiting like a time-bomb, I wasn't in control.

It took me over an hour to get there, and by the time I did, I was exhausted. I was thirsty and hungry, but I was too scared to go into any establishment and get myself something to eat or a bottle of water to drink. I couldn't live the rest of my life like this, in exile so I didn't hurt anyone. There had to be a way to get rid of this...curse.

It dawned on me that I'd lived my entire life thinking I had one curse, and when I'd got rid of it, I'd got myself another one.

I bit my lip and I mulled it over. If that asshole had never made me snort spells just to get a kick out of torturing me, this wouldn't be happening today. How was it possible that my life was still dictated by the dead dhampir?

I'd thought with him dead, my life would be back on track. I could fall in love, maybe have a family, make something out of my life, but I couldn't do any of those things or enjoy them while I was a walking danger. Finally, I reached the bridge in Camden and walked under it where Mother Red Cap lived. I didn't have a spell, and even if I did, I wouldn't have been able to use it, but I was hoping she could still hear me and let me in.

"Mother Red Cap, please open the door. I need to talk to you. It's important," I said and waited.

Nothing changed. No door appeared on the wall. No water started to boil. I remembered the first time we'd visited it had taken her a few good minutes to let us in; maybe that's what was happening now. I punched the wall, hoping she could hear it as a knock, but the wall was thick and barely anything other than a quiet thump was heard.

That was fine. Magic didn't work the same way as I'd thought. Perhaps she could still hear me, and this was just a test.

"Mother Red Cap, please let me in. I wouldn't have come to you if I had a choice."

A couple passed by and giggled, pointing at me as if I was a drunk that had had one too many drinks. I guess I was talking to a wall and waiting for an answer. Couldn't blame them. It was better being a crazy drunk than a timebomb. I had to do something.

"Mother Red, open this fucking door. I need to talk to you," I shouted and kicked the wall for good measure.

Of course, nothing changed. Why would it? Why would my life be made easier?

"I'm begging you, open the door. I don't know what I'll do if you don't." The words barely left my mouth before the tears took over me, and I had to turn around and steady myself on the railing.

I wasn't one to cry, especially not easily like that. I'd just been through hell, and it seemed that my return had never been secured. I was still stuck even if I had good company.

The thought of losing Caleb, of doing something to hurt him and little Nora, I couldn't live with myself. I also couldn't imagine having a life without him. He had given me mine back, but what was it worth without him?

My stomach rumbled, and I felt sick at the thought. The tears wouldn't stop, and I leaned over the water as my sick exploded. With it, dust came out. Magical dust that settled over the patch of the canal before it sunk and mixed with the water.

I heard a bolting noise behind me, and I turned to find the door on the wall.

"Finally," I said and pushed it open. I found myself in the corridor lit by torches with only one way to go. Straight ahead. I ran until I came to the wooden door, the last thing between me and the sage witch behind it.

She was sitting in the middle, by the fire pit, and she seemed to be gazing inside the flames, looking for answers to questions I wasn't privy to.

"Mother Red, thank you for letting me in."

She cocked her head and glanced at me.

"Come and sit, my child."

I walked to the middle and stepped down to sit a few feet away from her.

"Don't sit all the way over there. Come closer," she said and patted the space next to her.

She hadn't been this friendly before, but I thought nothing of it. I got up and sat down next to her. Before my ass hit the cushion, she turned around and grabbed me by the throat.

"Never do this again. There's a reason I've survived hundreds of years, and it wasn't because I'd let any old beggar into my den. Do you understand? You've just put me at risk by doing this."

I didn't know what I'd done wrong. I'd done just what Caleb had, sans offering a spell to her unless you counted my remnants as one. It hadn't been my intention to put her at risk or to piss her off. I needed her help.

"You came to me in the middle of the day, shouting outside my house. The mortals might not realize I exist, but those looking for me do. Do you understand? You put my life at risk because you need help with yours. That's not okay, Wade. It's not okay." She removed her hand from my throat.

Dammit. I forgot she could read minds. I had to be careful what I thought of in her presence. Especially if I wanted her to help me.

"What do you need from me?" she asked, and I could still detect the irritation in her voice.

"I'm really sorry. I wasn't thinking straight. It won't happen again."

She nodded in understanding.

"I know you're new to this world, but you need to think about the consequences of your actions."

"That's exactly why I am here. It seems that the magic I used to inhale is coming back."

"What do you mean coming back?"

"It means the spells I've used are somehow activating and putting people around me in danger. I was in bed with Caleb, and I nearly set him on fire, and then I was in the elevator and I almost choked myself with those vines that came out of nowhere. I'm afraid to go anywhere or do anything in case I hurt someone. I need your help."

"That's highly unusual. I've met people who used spells as a drug before, and it never, ever came back to activate. Especially since you don't know the spellwords, and you're not a witch. I can't understand why this is happening." She turned to look at me, this time with less fire in her eyes and more compassion.

"Caleb thinks it's because of the ley lines surging," I said, and her eyes widened.

"Of course. The surge. If that's what it is, there's nothing I can do to stop it. There's a reason why the ley lines have been sealed for centuries, and that is because they contain uncontrollable magic. If that's what's happening, you have to ride it out."

"No, I couldn't do that. I would be risking every-one's lives."

"Magic is emotional. If you're scared of hurting anyone, just try to control what you're feeling, and perhaps—I can't stress this enough—perhaps it might not happen again. But I believe riding it out is your only solution."

So this was it. I would have to live the rest of my life with another curse.

Fuck. My. Life.

FIVE
CALEB

After everything that happened in my house, I had to find out how I could help Wade, and if that meant doing what Graham wanted me to do, so be it.

Looking into the surge reports, there seemed to be a lot of aligning data between cases. There were many witches under Graham's protection now, which I wasn't happy about, but there were also reports of magical happenings without a witch attached to them. It was simply as if a bunch of witches had come into their powers, caused a scene, and then two seconds later they were off the grid. None of it made much sense, and I couldn't understand what was happening.

"My God! What are you doing in the dark? You scared the living crap out of me," Lorelai exclaimed when she entered the cafe a little after six.

I couldn't blame her for being shocked to see me. I

was usually the one late to arrive. I hated waking up early, but after what had happened two days ago, I couldn't get any sleep.

"Sorry. I-I came over to study these reports. I didn't mean to startle you."

She approached me with her hand still on her chest, her eyes pinned on mine.

"Startle? Try scared shitless."

I furrowed my brows and looked at her.

"I thought you had a good sense of smell."

"And? Do you think I was concentrating on who was in the shop while it was still closed? My mind was busy."

"Busy? What's occupying your mind at this time of the day, El?" I asked, but she didn't give in.

"None of your fucking business. What are those reports looking like? Any clue yet?" she asked and looked at the case files in front of me.

"No, not really. All these incidents and fledgling witches going off-grid. I don't know what to think."

Lorelai sat down opposite me and cocked her head, her eyes narrowing over the case files.

"If they're new witches and they've got no clue what's going on in the witch world, how would they know how to go off-grid?" she asked.

"That is the question. It's as if there is someone helping them, but none of the high council members are taking responsibility, which doesn't say much considering most of them are big-shot lawyers."

"And murderers. Let's not forget that," Lorelai added.

"Trust me. I couldn't even if I wanted to. I don't know what's happening, El. What do you think?"

She shrugged.

"Are there any witches that have left the coven and are doing their own thing? Like starting their own coven maybe?"

"No, Graham gave me the files of all the witches that have left the coven on bad terms, and the majority have moved out of London. A lot of them seem to have gone to the States actually."

"I can ask around the Nightcrawlers. Maybe they've seen something."

"If you can do that, that would be amazing."

"Of course. Anything for you." She winked and got up. "Now get your ass off the chair and help me open up the shop."

———

After the morning rush and just when I was about to leave to take Nora out for a walk, Wade showed up at work looking miserable and in need of good company.

"I'm not staying long. I just wanted to see you," he said to me and greeted me with a kiss.

"Don't be stupid. I'm here. If anything happens, I can stop it."

"What if it's something you can't control?"

I pursed my lips and raised my eyebrow.

"Excuse me, have you met me?" I said, and that made him chuckle.

"I have. And I'm so glad I have."

Even when he was depressed, he knew just the right thing to tell me to make me melt inside. Being free of Christian's control was doing wonders for him.

"Walk me home, will you?" I asked and opened the door to leave the cafe.

"See you tomorrow, Caleb. Bye, scumbag," Lorelai said, and Wade nodded at her before closing the door behind him.

"Is she ever going to change her mind about me?"

I grinned and looked at him.

"Lorelai is a special lady. And she knows how to hold a grudge, okay? So don't keep on hoping, but it could happen."

He seemed to like what I'd said and nodded in appreciation.

We walked on the busy streets of London just when all the office workers were about to go on their lunch breaks, and Wade started to panic, looking at every person that came near him. I looked for the nearest side street and took us through it; I couldn't stand seeing him like this. Living his life in fear of hurting someone and resorting to solitude because of it.

I laced my fingers around his and gave his hand a squeeze.

"Everything is going to be alright, okay? I promise you."

He paused to look at me and only reciprocated with half a smile back.

"I believe you. But until then, what do I do?"

"I don't know, Wade. But locking yourself away from everyone is not the solution."

When we reached my front door, he leaned in to give me a kiss and to say goodbye, but I held onto him.

"Walk Nora with me," I begged him.

He leaned back and looked at me as if I was a lunatic.

"Caleb, I can't. What if something happens when I'm with her and I hurt her."

"Don't forget Nora is an ancient creature that can never die. But even if something happens, I'm here. I can stop you." I put my hand on his chest and let some of my confidence flow through my hand over to him.

His body relaxed under my touch, and he succumbed to my little boost.

"I'll go get her. Why don't you wait out here?" I said and ran up the stairs. Five minutes later, we were back on the ground floor and Nora had just woken up, so she kept busy with the toys in her pram.

"Any more incidents?" I asked him.

He shook his head and put his hands in his pockets.

"Any luck with your search?" he asked.

"Not much. Nothing really. All I've got is a lot of

reports with no leads. Many witches that were ignited after that night on the rooftop have gone missing, and I don't know how or why."

He flinched at that and stopped walking.

"What do you mean they've gone missing? Someone's abducting them?"

I shrugged. "Either that or they're going into hiding. Despite how many weeks have passed since the big blast of energy, there are still new reports coming in every day. This means that your outbursts were, in fact, connected to the ley lines and nothing to do with you," I told him, thinking this would reassure him, but it only made the crease in his eyebrows deeper.

"Mother Red Cap said she couldn't stop them. She said the ley lines are very strong, ancient magic, and that no one can stop it. So how are we gonna stop me?"

I reached for his hand and squeezed it.

"Wade, sweetheart, don't take this the wrong way, but the ley lines are unstoppable, not you."

He laughed. It was a good look on him. I liked seeing it back on his face.

"You're right. The spells I used were just that. Spells. There's no way they have anything to do with the force of the ley lines."

"Exactly."

We continued walking and entered Weavers Fields park where lots of people were sitting on benches or on the grass eating sandwiches for their lunch break, and lots more people walking their dogs.

We walked past a couple, one of whose faces I recognized. We'd worked together in the past on one of my cases for Graham and the high council. I couldn't quite remember his name, but he was a well-respected witch in the community, so I nodded hello to him.

My kindness was met with apathy. Both he and his girlfriend flinched, and the girl even went as far as to make a disgusted face in our direction. After we'd walked past them and I'd decided to completely ignore their rudeness, I heard her make a sound and turned in time to see her spit on the spot we'd just walked on.

"Hey, what's your fucking problem?" Wade asked, and I had to give his forearm a little jolt of calm to make sure he didn't have another incident.

"Witch hunters for one thing," the woman said and spat again, this time aiming right for Wade's face.

"Who the fuck do you think you are?" I growled and walked closer to her after putting the brakes on Nora's pram.

She smiled in a sly, uptight way. This bitch thought she was better than me.

"That's all he deserves. You deserve worse for sleeping with him," she whispered in my face, and her boyfriend took her hand and pulled her towards him.

I laughed in her face.

"At least I know where my boyfriend puts his dick. Do you know what holes yours does?" I knew it was a low blow, but I didn't care. She'd spat in my Wade's face.

Her boyfriend's eyes widened, and his face went red, staring at me, but he dragged her away from us without another word.

"Did you really sleep with him?" Wade asked as soon as they were out of earshot.

I turned to him and saw him wipe his face with the hem of his shirt.

"Of course not. Did you see his face?" I laughed. "But the stripper incubi in Soho probably have a different story."

Wade chuckled and turned back to Nora.

"Are you okay?" I asked him.

"I'm fine," he said, not sounding convincing. "Are you?"

Was I okay? I was fucking pissed. How dare anyone tell me how to live my life. When the fuck did they get to decide who I slept with and why? Who were they to pass judgment on me for sleeping with a witch hunter?

"No, I'm not okay, but I'll be okay," I told him and grabbed Nora's pram to continue the walk.

I wasn't going to let those assholes dictate my life. And if they thought I was going to be afraid of a little confrontation, they were sorely mistaken.

It had taken me years to find a tribe I wanted to belong to and that wanted me, and I'd thought being part of the coven would do that for me. But if that's the attitude I was going to get for falling for a beautiful man who had made mistakes in his past like everyone else I knew, including myself, then perhaps the coven wasn't my tribe at all.

It was fine. If I couldn't belong to any other tribe, I could make my own. And I had one already. Annabel, Nora, Lorelai, and Hew. And Wade, of course. They were all my tribe, and I was going to do everything in my power to protect them.

Six

Wade

I didn't like going behind Caleb's back, but I couldn't put this on him. I had to find a way to help the situation without putting any more pressure on him. After what had happened at the park the other day, I couldn't let him get more involved with me. I wasn't going to break up with him because of what the witches said, but I could at least keep my business to myself.

He might wake up one day and realize he was giving up everything he had for me. I didn't want him to do that. He'd had a life before me, and I couldn't expect him to sacrifice it all for me.

I waited for him to leave early in the morning, watched him from a fruit stall, and once he was out of sight, I approached his front door. I knew it was early, and I hoped Annabel was not going to be too upset with me for waking her up, but I knocked on the door.

A few moments later, Annabel barreled down the stairs and opened the front door. She was wearing slippers and bunny-print pajamas. She didn't look like the strong Annabel who didn't take any bullshit. She looked like a normal girl. I knew she wasn't.

"Did you forget your keys again?" she said, and then she saw me and placed her hand on her hip to give me a look I was more used to.

"What do you want?" she asked.

"I'm sorry to wake you—"

"You didn't wake me. Nora did," she said and stepped aside to let me in.

"You look annoyed. Did Nora stay up all night again?"

She started climbing the stairs, and I followed.

"No. If she was back to her old, adult self, I would kill her for doing this to me. But no, she won't let us sleep. I think she's taking revenge on Caleb, and I am taking the thick of it."

I couldn't imagine having to stay at home all day with a baby for five years. No wonder Annabel was upset.

"What do you do? Do you work?" I asked her.

It had never occurred to me to ask. I'd just assumed she stayed at home looking after Nora while Caleb went to work for the high council. It probably had been presumptuous of me to assume she was staying at home because she had no job other than looking after Nora, but surely she wouldn't let Caleb, or any man, dictate her life. I didn't know her well, but that much I knew about her.

"I'm a graphic designer. Why are you asking? I don't have any positions."

I was about to tell her I wasn't asking for a job when I noticed the smirk on her face.

"Annabel, are you actually warming up to me?" I asked, and the smile disappeared.

"Don't push it, mister," she said and opened the door at the top of the stairs and walked to the kitchen to put the kettle on to boil.

"Tea all right with you?" she asked and took two cups out of the cupboard.

Tea was her signature drink, as I'd come to learn. Annabel had this special blend that was the perfect companion to any sort of conversation. Whether you were hurt and in need of a friend, or just having a lively chat with a friend, her tea was complimentary to everything. So it was no wonder that I accepted the offer.

I sat at the dining table and waited for her to sit with me. When she did, she offered me a cup with a cartoon mouse printed on it.

"What do you want to talk about? I can't imagine I will be much help, but I am curious what you think I can do for you."

I curled my fingers around the mug and warmed my hands, giving her an innocent smile.

"How do you know I need help with something?"

"Well, I don't imagine you came to my house at six

in the morning to ask me how I'm feeling and if I need a night out."

"You got me. But really, are you okay? Do you need a night out?"

She rolled her eyes, but I could detect a grin trying to make an appearance.

"I'm fine, Wade. Nora may be driving me crazy, but I have been doing this for years, so I'm good. It's your boyfriend you should worry about."

"Why? Has he said something?"

Annabel shook her head. "He doesn't have to. I know him pretty well. And I know that he is not himself. He's probably blaming himself for what's happening to the witches."

"I know. I told him it's not his fault, but—"

"It's not your fault, either. I think you both are forgetting that monster manipulated both of you. You actually saved lives, okay?"

It meant a lot coming from her, but I couldn't help feeling that this was a pep talk rather than the truth.

"That's why I'm here," I told her.

"What? You gonna try to guilt-trip me into thinking this is my fault?" She chuckled.

I shook my head. "No. I need help from someone who knows their magic shit. I need to talk to Graham."

Annabel looked at me as if I'd said the devil's name in a church. She put her tea down and pierced me with her eyes.

"Why on earth would you want to do that?"

"Because there's something going on, and I need his expertise."

"Did you forget that he is a douchebag who betrayed hundreds of witches for you guys to hunt and kill?"

I shook my head.

"Good, I just wanted to check. Have you lost your mind?"

"I need to talk to him."

"Why don't you go to that Mother Red, whatever her name is, the one Nora sent you to? Why do you want to talk to that asshole?"

"I tried that, and she was unable to help. Caleb has told me about Graham's power, and, I don't know, maybe he can help."

"Help with what?"

"Nothing."

"It wouldn't have anything to do with a burned bed, would it?" She glanced in the direction of Caleb's room.

I shrugged. "Maybe."

"What's going on?"

I wanted to tell her, but I didn't want to freak her out. She loved Nora as much as Caleb did, but unlike him, she wasn't a witch, and she couldn't stop me if anything happened. I was actually putting her in danger by being here. But I didn't know where else to turn. I didn't know what else to try. I had to do something.

"I just need to talk to him. Can you please tell me where he lives?"

———

It took a few phone calls and a lot of convincing, but when the door finally opened at Graham's house, I was met with what I expected. Disdain and a little bit of hatred. Or a lot of hatred. I didn't know. This guy was a mystery to me. He had let the high council take advantage of his power and his position, yet he was upset about me killing them, so who knew what he felt like.

"What can I do for you, witch hunter?"

I liked a man that cut to the chase as much as the next person, and I couldn't say I expected anything less, but I wasn't going to have this conversation outside.

"This is a delicate matter. Can I come in?" I asked, making sure to add enough authority in my voice to let him know that I didn't care who he was and what he thought of me.

"Of course," he said with an extra bit of joviality in his voice that was nowhere to be seen in his face.

I walked into what looked like a mansion to me. My preference had always been apartments. I'd never been much into houses or anything too big, but this was something else. Caleb had told me Graham was loaded, and the area he lived in should have given me a hint of how rich he was, but I did not expect a house like this.

Every surface was covered in either gold, silver, or granite. Every wooden surface seemed to be ancient and preserved. And every trinket seemed to contain a gemstone, although knowing him, they were probably spells.

He led me through the hallway into the lounge and offered me a seat on a chaise longue that could have belonged to Marie Antoinette from the looks of it. He sat in an armchair opposite, looking regal and imposing. He knew how to play mind games very well. I could give him that.

"You have to understand I am only doing this for Caleb," he said.

"I know. So am I. That's why I wanted to meet you."

"What's going on? Why do you need my help?"

I laced my fingers together and thought of how to phrase what I needed to ask.

Had I made a mistake coming to him? Was I better off riding it out like Mother Red Cap had suggested? Did I really need the help of a conspirator to murder?

"I can't go into specifics, but do you think you'd be able to create a spell to block other spells from going off?"

He narrowed his eyes and stared right down at me. He stayed quiet for a few moments before he actually spoke.

"If I'm going to make a spell for you, I need to know exactly what it's for."

That was a fair point. Too bad I couldn't tell him.

"Let's say you had a witch who didn't know how to control her natural power. And you needed to protect her and everyone else around her. What spell would you give her to make her power harmless?"

Caleb had explained to me how Graham's powers worked. It was all about altering and manipulating energy. Which was why he could create a spell from anything, unlike Mother Red Cap and other witches who were also dabbling in alchemy. Usually, you needed a selection of ingredients to create a spell, but for Graham, it was as simple as putting together two grains of salt, and he could create any sort of spell he desired. Of course, he had his limitations, but according to Caleb, more often than not, those limitations were easily manipulated with some proper alchemy.

"I would train her hard until she dropped. I wouldn't cast a spell on her."

I chuckled.

"Good one. And I would never kill a witch," I said. "You can't fool me, and I really need your help. So cut the crap."

My cursing seemed to put him on edge as he leaned back in his chair and crossed his arms in front of his chest protectively.

"I might be able to craft something. But how do you plan on activating it? You're not a witch."

"Leave me to worry about that."

"How much?" he asked.

"How much, what?"

"How much are you willing to pay for this spell?"

I had to bite down the urge to laugh in his face. Was he being serious? Did he actually think I'd pay to use his services?

"I'll tell you what. Let's call it even for what you did to Caleb. How does that sound?"

He didn't like the answer, and it showed in the way his posture changed again. He crossed his legs and took the glasses off the crown of his head and put them on.

"Fine. You can sit here while I get it ready," he said and rushed to get up. "Don't touch anything," he hissed before disappearing into his kitchen, and I was left alone.

I didn't know how long it would take, and I wasn't going to sit on my ass while he prepared it, so I got up and paced around the room, taking a closer look at his decor.

I approached the mantelpiece where numerous frames were placed on the shelf over it. There were pictures of other people posing with Graham. At first, I assumed it was his family until I came up against one of Caleb. He was much younger, and his hair looked different. I almost didn't recognize him. I knew him as the silver-haired dude with the nose and eyebrow piercings who had stolen my heart. The guy staring at me in the picture was just a kid. A kid with a shaved head and glasses.

Was this how he'd looked when I'd met him before, when he'd gone undercover in the BLADE force? Was this who he had been before he'd erased his memory of us to protect a secret?

Sometimes I wished I hadn't made the decision to forget everything Christian had made me do. Sometimes I wished I'd chosen to remember even if I couldn't handle it. I wished I could remember Caleb and me. Remember falling in love with him for the first time. How did I feel back then? Did I freak out because I was attracted to another guy? Or did it feel as normal as it did now?

Sure, it hadn't come easy to me this time around, but maybe old me found it even easier to be with Caleb. Had I always been attracted to men and had Christian made me forget that?

That had never crossed my mind. Could he have manipulated me that much that I had changed orientation? Surely I would remember that. But then again, I didn't remember much, and the things I did, I wasn't entirely certain if they were true. Sometimes it was better to live with lies than to know the truth, right?

Caleb looked happy in the picture. Even if Graham had committed unspeakable crimes, he had given him a gift. He had given him the witch community and a cause. Something to live for. He'd made him belong to something, to a coven, finding some sort of stability in his life after everything he had been through. And I was taking all of this away from him simply by being with him. How could I ever make it up to him and to everyone else I'd hurt? Could I even do that?

And when would Caleb realize he didn't really love me and that his coven meant more to him than being with me? Because that was bound to happen. How could he love me?

"I said don't touch my stuff," Graham shouted behind me, and I jumped.

I hadn't even heard him walking in, so I almost dropped the frame I was holding, but I steadied it in my hands and put it back in its place. I sat down on the couch again.

"Is it ready?"

"It is," he said and opened his hand to reveal a green stone.

I reached for it, but before I could grab it, he closed his fist around it.

"Before I give it to you, tell me, why do you need it?"

I stared at him, unwilling to give an answer. He waited for one nonetheless, but I wasn't going to back down.

"Fine," he said and opened his palm to give me access to the stone.

I took it in my hand and inspected it. It looked real. Certainly felt real. Thankfully, I didn't feel the urge to ground it to a powder and snort it. I'd take that as a win.

"What's the spellword?"

"Protect," he said slowly, as if it wasn't a spellword at all but a threat to me.

"You're not going to regret this."

He sat down and crossed his legs.

"Something tells me I am."

I stood up, about to leave, when I caught a glimpse of the frame again.

"Can I ask you something?"

His eyes narrowed and he didn't blink.

"Has there ever been another witch hunter that found out the truth and decided to change?"

He answered almost immediately.

"Never."

Was that true? There had never been another witch hunter to find out the truth and make a change in their life? I hoped it wasn't.

"All the terrible things you did for Christian. How can you live with yourself?"

His frown deepened, and his mouth opened in shock.

"How dare you—" he started, but I cut him off before he could continue.

"I'm not asking to make you feel bad. I'm asking for advice."

"What advice?"

"How can you live with yourself after everything you've done?"

He pursed his lips and his nostrils flared.

"I did what I had to do to protect the many. That's how," he shouted.

"But I killed blindly. Sometimes I even enjoyed it."

"I can't help you with that," he yelled.

I nodded and squeezed the spell before putting it in the inside pocket of my jacket.

"I guess..." he muttered behind me, and I turned.

I caught him rolling his eyes and taking a deep breath.

"At least you can live with yourself because you weren't in control of your actions," he said, and his honesty made me feel sorry for him.

As much as he was trying to hide it, he felt terrible about what he'd done. And I could definitely relate to that.

I thanked him and left his house. I could almost feel the energy blasting me out of his home, as if he'd put up the security the moment I left.

When I came out of the front garden and looked behind me, the house I saw was not the house I'd been in. The mansion I had walked out of was now derelict.

Clever man, protecting himself. Now I could protect others from myself too.

I decided to rent a bike to take home. At least that offered some sort of security and safety from harming others and didn't mean I was exhausting myself, and it got to my apartment block a little after eight in the evening.

I rode the elevator, this time without any chance encounters with Mrs. Weatherby, and entered my apartment. As soon as I'd shut the door, I heard a knock.

"Speak of the devil," I thought to myself and turned to open my door.

Mrs. Weatherby often knocked on the door to borrow things even after I'd told her a hundred times I didn't cook.

It wasn't Mrs. Weatherby.

Lloyd was standing on my doorstep. My partner up until four weeks ago. But it wasn't just a social visit. He was bleeding. He had a big cut across his chest, and his eye was bruised. Blood was dried under his nose, and his left leg was twisted.

"Lloyd, what happened to you?" I asked and immediately put his arm around my neck and helped him inside the flat.

He yelped in pain with every step that we took until we reached the couch, and I helped ease him onto it.

"It's—" he started to say but choked on blood. I helped him turn sideways so he could spit it out and clear his throat. "It's Christian. He's back. And he's killed them all," he said, and the terror chilled my body. "He's killed all the Blades."

SEVEN
CALEB

"He's the man who tried to kill me. He tried to kill *you*. And you want me to listen to him?" I asked Wade when I arrived at his apartment.

He'd sounded so panicked when he was on the phone, I'd literally dropped everything and raced to his house. The taxi I had taken had cost me a fortune, and after discovering what had got him so upset, I wasn't sure it was worth the cost.

Lloyd Jenkins. Witch hunter and asshole extraordinaire. The man who'd chased after us the entire time Wade and I had been trying to swap hearts and find out the truth about the high council murders. The man that had chased us down the streets of Whitechapel to kill us. And Wade wanted me to help heal him.

"Look, Caleb. Lloyd has been lied to all his life too.

Okay? He may not have been controlled by Christian, but he was still told all the crap they taught us at the force. He needs a second chance too. And he doesn't have much time left," Wade begged me, his eyes red and swollen.

I couldn't understand why, but he really cared about this dude. And if Wade cared about someone, then I cared about them too. That didn't mean I had to like them.

"Fine. But I'm charging him."

Wade tugged at my shoulder and gave it a squeeze.

"I'll pay you," Wade said.

I sighed and let go of him. Lloyd had been lying in Wade's bed, which meant both of us would have to go bed shopping if we were to have a decent night's sleep ever again. Wade had tied cloths and T-shirts around Lloyd's wounds to stop the blood flow until I got here. The man was barely conscious but still flinched when I sat down on the bed next to him.

"He-he-a...witch," he groaned, a barely audible sound.

"Well done, Sherlock. You win," I said and removed a green crystal off my bracer and placed it over him.

I didn't normally carry healing stones with me, and I didn't keep many at home, just enough to stock the first aid kit, but since both Wade and I almost lost our lives, repeatedly, over the span of three days, I'd made sure to get enough to avoid a recurrence.

I couldn't use Nora anymore. Since she'd sacrificed herself twice for me, and I'd made a promise to myself and to Annabel that I'd never use her abilities ever again, not even for small things.

"*Cura*," I said, and the crystal exploded all over Lloyd, encasing him in green iridescent dust like a fancy Egyptian mummy, and within seconds, his body absorbed it, leaving no trace of his wounds.

"What the fuck did you just do to me?" Lloyd said as soon as he felt well enough to sit up.

"You're welcome, asshole," I told him.

He had just cost me four hundred pounds, and he wasn't even grateful. Why did Wade even like this guy? He was a puny little bastard.

"Lloyd, he just saved your life, idiot. The least you can do is be grateful," Wade shouted at him.

Lloyd grimaced and edged away from my touch before giving me a half-assed thanks.

"I thought you'd be done with him after everything that happened," he said. "You lost your job because of him."

Wade laughed. "Oh, Lloyd, you don't know anything, do you? Come on. I'll make coffee, and you can tell us what happened."

He grabbed Lloyd by the back of his neck and pushed him in the direction of the living room. Wade gave me a quick glance and an eye roll and disappeared next door while I stood up and inspected the bed.

Was it salvageable? I'd used cleaning spells before,

but Graham was a bastard and charged a fortune for them, and I wasn't asking him for any favors again.

Ah, fuck it. I'd buy us a new one. Maybe one of those new memory-foam beds with the human name should do it. And I could put a protective spell around it so it never got dirty. Hopefully, the spell wouldn't even be needed, but you never knew in this world.

I joined them in the living room where Lloyd sat on the couch and Wade was over at his kitchen brewing an espresso for the asshat I'd just saved.

"Tell us what happened. Christian is back?" I asked him, and he glared at me as soon as I addressed him.

"I'm not talking to a witch."

I crossed my arms in front of my chest and stared right at him.

"Listen, you little douchebag. If it weren't for your friend and me, Christian would have become an unstoppable monster and would have killed all witches."

"Good. Then we'd be rid of your scum."

"And who do you think he'd go after next? Once he'd got his fix from all the witches? Oh...wait. He already has." Lloyd looked away from me and bit his lip. "The problem is, he should be dead. If he isn't, we've got a problem. So talk, for fuck's sake."

Wade approached with a cup and handed it to Lloyd.

"You can trust Caleb. He's a good guy," he said and put his hand on the small of my back.

The look on Lloyd's face said it all. Not only was he shocked Wade was still working with "the enemy," but he was also in awe that Wade was touching me in such an intimate way.

"Fine," he finally said and looked down at his coffee as if he was looking for liquid courage.

And it turned out he did need it because what he had to say wasn't easy.

"I don't know where to start."

I didn't want to be the cliché guy that said from the beginning, but that's exactly what I did.

"I don't know where the beginning is. When you and Winston were dismissed, Carter cracked the whip on the rest of us. Anyone who had been close to you guys was put under the microscope to find out if there were any other traitors. But everyone in the force wanted to know what happened to you, and most importantly what happened to Christian.

"So Carter told us everything. He told us about the Nightcrawlers and what Christian truly was, and then he said that you and Winston stopped him with the help of a witch. He said the only reason he wasn't going to go after you was because of what you achieved but warned us against witches and Nightcrawlers.

"We've all been assigned classes to catch up on all the shit Christian kept from us. To be honest, most of us feel that's all we've been doing. Witches trails have gone cold since you left, but there have been numerous incidents of magical activity around London."

"The ley line surges," I mumbled.

Lloyd shrugged.

"Yeah, whatever that's supposed to mean. Everyone was starting to feel deflated, and there had been whispers about the force being better under Marlowe's direction even though he was evil."

I huffed. "Evil doesn't begin to cover it. Did Carter tell you that Christian had performed blood magic on Wade and his brother that made him control their every action, every thought, every memory?" I yelled. Not at Lloyd in particular, but everything he represented.

"What?" he asked.

Wade dismissed the subject as if it was nothing.

"It's a long story. I'll tell you later. We've got more important stuff to talk about now," Wade said. "Tell us about the attack."

"The attack." Lloyd nodded and looked at his coffee again. "He came out of nowhere. He didn't look like himself. He was furious. His eyes were—I don't know how to describe it—like, possessed. Some of us didn't know how to react. If he was back, did that mean Carter had lied to us?

"Then Carter came out of his office and ordered everyone to arm themselves, but it all happened in a flash. Carter was the first to be killed. Christian put a sword right through his heart. Then, all hell broke loose. We tried to kill him, but nothing seemed to faze him. I'd never seen him like that before. So inhuman."

The emptiness in Lloyd's eyes told me he'd been scarred for life. I knew first-hand what it was like to witness such destruction. I felt for the guy.

"He never was human. He hasn't been in a very long time," I said, and Lloyd nodded.

"He killed so many. I-I had to..." Lloyd welled up, and he stopped to sniff and compose himself.

"Whatever you had to do, you had to. To survive," Wade told him.

"I pretended I was dead," Lloyd admitted. "While he killed everyone, I pretended I was down for good. I..."

He broke down in tears and finally let a side of the real Lloyd show. I liked this side of him more than the hateful asshole he had been earlier.

"He would have killed you if you hadn't. There was no way you could stop him, Lloyd. There was no way anyone could." Wade sat down next to him to put his arm around his ex-partner.

"I could have tried. I—"

"No. You couldn't. You'd be dead if you had, and we wouldn't know any of this," I said, and he hesitantly raised his eyes to meet mine.

"If we can't stop him, how can you?"

I wanted to tell him I was powerful enough to end him once and for all. I wanted to tell him that the witches could get rid of him for good. But I couldn't in good conscience do that. So, instead of lying, I shrugged.

"Don't know yet, but I'll find a way."

"Lloyd, was there anyone else who survived?" Wade asked, but right then a loud knock disturbed the tension in the room.

"Are you expecting anyone?" I asked as we both jumped and gestured for Lloyd to stay quiet.

Wade shook his head slowly, and I tiptoed to the door, careful not to leave a shadow underneath the crack.

"It's just Winston," I said and opened up.

Winston barged in with Hew in tow, and Lloyd stood up to get a better view of both of them.

"Another witch? What is going on with you two?" he said, looking at Hew and his jewel-loaded choker.

"I heard what happened at HQ. What are you doing here?" Winston said to Lloyd, decidedly ignoring his comment.

"Lloyd was there when it happened," Wade said.

Hew stepped closer to Lloyd and inspected his blood-soaked clothes.

"How did you survive? No one else did," Hew said, and Lloyd flinched away from him. "Also, I'm only half-witch, if you must know."

"How do you know no one else survived?" Wade asked.

"After we heard, we went to HQ, and Hew spoke with everyone," Winston said.

That made sense.

"What do you mean spoke with everyone? Everyone died," Lloyd yelled.

Hew put his hands in front of him and gestured for Lloyd to keep it down.

"Calm your tits, man. I spoke to their spirits. I'm a psychic."

Lloyd took a few steps back and collapsed on the sofa.

"You'd think I told him I was the president of the United States with that kind of reaction," Hew said and rolled his eyes.

"He faked his own death so he could escape," I told Hew. "Did none of the dead Blades see Lloyd leave the force?"

Hew shook his head.

"I think they were all a tad too shocked after what happened that they didn't get a chance. Half of them wouldn't even talk to me because they thought they were still alive and I was an intruder," he said and laughed. "Idiots."

"Hey!" Lloyd shouted. "Have some respect for the fallen heroes, will ya?"

Hew crossed his arms and smirked.

"Fallen heroes? Puh-lease. Catch up with the times, dude. You've been feeding a dhampir all these years, and your best hunters have switched sides. That should tell you how much of a hero you are," Hew said and raised an eyebrow when Lloyd turned to look at Winston.

"You're gay now too?" he asked him.

Winston looked like a deer in headlights. I didn't know how much progress the two had made, and at the end of the day, it didn't matter if he was ready to be out as long as they were both happy and working through everything together.

"I meant sides in the war, but yeah, Winston's gay too." Hew chuckled, and Winston huffed at his comment.

"Bi, thank you, and that's not the point right now. We've got agents too scared to do anything, fearing for their lives."

"I thought everyone died," I said.

Winston turned to me. "Only the ones on shift, thankfully. But that's, like, half the force."

"Christian might come after them. They need to stay low," I said.

Winston nodded. "That's exactly what I was thinking."

Hew sat on the stool by the kitchen counter and rubbed his chin.

"Why would he come after the Blades? He spent years shaping you into his minion—"

"Hey!" Lloyd shouted at him.

"Whatever you want to call it, you were doing his bidding. Get over it. He built your force. He went out of his way to make sure no one cared about Night-crawlers, and you only went after witches and their magic. He trained you to be expert killers. Why would he turn on you?"

"Because they turned on him? Maybe?" I offered. "My question is how the fuck is he still alive? I activated his life crystal and killed him on the roof of the White Tower. He was bound to that crystal. How the hell did he survive it?"

Hew shrugged.

"The ley lines?" he said. "When you died in that pentacle, maybe he fed on the ley lines making his life crystal redundant? But I don't know."

Wade stepped into our conversation both physically and verbally.

"Do you think maybe he's connected to those missing witches? Maybe they're not going underground. Maybe he's feeding on them and disposing of them."

That was a possibility. And if it was true, then I had no freaking idea how to stop him.

"I think we need to freshen up on our knowledge about dhampirs," I said.

EIGHT

WADE

The surviving agents all went into hiding, Lloyd included, and for the rest of the week, all four of us did our research.

Winston and I had a lot to learn about the Nightcrawler world, and I couldn't believe that even the force had caught up when I still didn't know half the things Caleb was talking about. So, while Hew and Caleb researched about dhampirs, Winston and I did all the Nightcrawler 101 that we'd missed out on all these years.

"How is it going with you two?" I asked Winston a few days into our hardcore reading sessions during a beer and pizza break.

Winston looked up and offered me a grimace.

"I don't know. Good, I guess. It's all so weird, you know. I know it's almost been a month, but it's hard to take it all in. Like, when I'm with him, I can't keep my hands off him, and I can't stand the thought of him getting hurt, and it's like everything makes sense. But as soon as he leaves, I miss him like crazy, and I don't know why."

I chuckled.

"Sounds a lot like you're in love."

He shrugged.

"Or it's that damn bonding that's causing all this," he said.

"Nah. That's exactly how I feel about Caleb."

He froze for a second, I assumed while he made sense of what I was telling him, and then he seemed to deflate like a worn out, over-rubbed penis.

"So, this is what it feels like, huh?" he said.

"What? You don't like it? Is it not what you expected?"

If it wasn't, I couldn't really blame him. Unlike me, he'd chosen to keep his distance from women while he'd thought his heart was cursed. The fact that Christian didn't loathe him like me had also helped keep his heart intact and his trauma at ease.

But he'd still suffered, and he knew all the details of what Christian had made him forget.

"No, it's...I don't know. It's better, I think. I mean, it's weird that it's with a guy, and fuck me, there's a lot to learn. Did you know what douching is?"

I shook my head.

"Me neither. Hew explained it to me, and fuck me, is it hard work. Like, I always thought dudes could just fuck whenever and wherever. But no. There's all the prep and toys—" He snapped his mouth shut, realizing what he'd said.

"Wait a minute. Toys?" I raised an eyebrow but kept my laughter in. For now.

"You haven't used toys?"

I shook my head, and he grimaced.

"Really? I expected Caleb to be into this kind of stuff," he said.

Well, maybe he was, but I wasn't going to tell him that we both liked playing rough with each other. That was for Caleb and me to know.

"So, what? You just fuck each other without easing into it?" he asked.

"I haven't... It's Caleb that usually..."

I shouldn't have felt awkward, but I'd never had such intimate chats with my brother, especially not about sex, or gay sex even, and I didn't know what to make of it.

We'd been denied a brotherly connection, surely a thing of Christian's doing, as Winston had found out. He'd liked to make us turn on each other every once in a while, just so that we didn't get close.

Winston clapped his hands and sat back on the couch, dropping a slice of pizza back in the box.

"Dude, what the fuck are you waiting for? You've got to try it."

I raised my eyebrow again, and he laughed.

"What?" he said. "You only live once, right? Unless

you're Caleb, I guess. I was scared at first, but it's nice once you get some...practice." He cleared his throat at the last word.

Was I really talking with my brother about anal? And was he really being open and nice about it when a few weeks ago he didn't want to be touched by Hew in any shape or form?

God, Hew must have been good in bed if he'd convinced Winston to bottom. It hadn't even crossed my mind to try it, and Caleb hadn't mentioned it, but then again, this last week we'd both been busy trying to find a way to stop Christian. Again.

Maybe he wanted to try and he was afraid to say so?

Nah. If there was one thing about Caleb, it was that he wasn't scared to speak his mind. Ever. Even when it was best to keep quiet.

"Anyway," I said in a desperate attempt to change the subject. "How's the muscle for hire thing going? Any takers yet?"

Winston pursed his lips and shook his head.

"No witches yet. They're all too scared of an ex-witch hunter. I can't blame them. But Hew is hoping things will change once they see we're trying to help. He's taken on a few cases for Nightcrawlers to try and smooth things over. He thinks it'll be easier to convince the Nightcrawlers, and once the witches see the good we do, they'll come to us too."

"How is that working?" I asked, knowing the answer already.

"Well, his brothers are hellbent on seeing me destroyed even if it means Hew will die too," he said as if it was a matter of throwing an out-of-date food item in the bin and not as if he was talking about life and death.

"Why the hell would they want that?"

"Things were already shit with his siblings. Considering he's one of the few half-witch, half-familiars to exist—" he started, but he'd already lost me.

"What do you mean? Aren't his siblings witches too?"

Caleb had tried to explain things to me, but when he was talking, it was hard to focus on his words. His lips were so damn irresistible.

"No. Their mother is. And she married a familiar that wasn't her mate before she met her true one. So, she had Hew, and he was born a half-breed. Then, when she met her mate, she had his siblings, but from a familiar–witch bond, your child is one or the other. Never both. Hew's considered a freak of nature. Which is why he was never close to his brothers. So you can imagine what they think of him now that he's bonded with a human."

Wow. I would never have known. I'd read some things about familiars and their shifting abilities, but never anything about their mating. Poor Hew. He had a lot on his plate. As if seeing dead people's spirits everywhere wasn't enough.

My phone pinged, and I turned to read the message from Caleb.

"Crap, I almost forgot," I said, springing up and grabbing my coat.

"What's going on?"

"Caleb and I are on babysitting duty tonight. I've got to go." Winston stood up. "Stay. Read up. It's fine, Win. You don't have to go."

He put his hands in his pockets and raised his shoulders.

"If you're sure."

I stepped around the coffee table and stood in front of him, taking both shoulders in my hands.

"Of course, idiot. You're my brother. Christian might have taken our bond away from us, but we're still brothers. And we're free of him now. We can be proper brothers again. I trust you."

His gaze moved from my stare.

"If only you knew what I'd done to you, you wouldn't."

"Whatever you've done, that wasn't you. This, right here, is you. And I trust you now. I'd trust you with my life," I said and took him in my arms. "Whatever we've done to each other is all in the past."

I felt his hands lifting up to hug me right back. It felt good being a brother again. It probably felt weird for Winston who didn't remember a life without

Christian's control, but I could. And we were in this shit together.

———

When I got to Caleb's house, Annabel opened the door. They were all sitting at the dining table. Annabel feeding Nora, and Caleb studying a book that looked as old as the house we were in, if not older.

"Hi, Wade. Are you ready for another sleepless night?" Annabel asked as soon as she saw me.

Caleb raised an eyebrow, but before he could say anything, she tutted.

"Not that kind of sleepless night, you slut. Honestly, do you ever not think about sex?"

"Uhm, excuse me, but I haven't had any in a week, so you can fuck off if you think you can victimize me like that. I'm deeply offended," Caleb fake-cried.

"Oh, shut up, you whore. You've gone on longer than that and you've been fine."

"Any luck?" I asked, interrupting the happy banter that both were enjoying way too much.

I stood behind Caleb and leaned over him to read from his book. The calligraphy on the page made everything look as if it was a different language, and I struggled to read anything.

"Nothing. It seems dhampirs really are rarer than blood diamonds because not much is written about them other than the basics," he said. "I've also looked into that binding spell Danielle's girlfriend performed on Christian, and it's conclusive that once the crystal is destroyed, so is the person. I can't understand why Christian is still alive."

"It must be the ley lines," Annabel said.

"Exactly, but there's no information anywhere about stopping those surges or on how to seal them back again."

Annabel stood and placed Nora over her chest, patting her back waiting for her to burp, although she already looked ready to sleep.

"Give it a rest for tonight. Watch a film. Rome wasn't built in a day, Caleb. Don't expect miracles."

Caleb slapped his hand on the table and let his body collapse onto it.

"I know, Ann. But the longer it takes, the more people get hurt. I'll just have to keep reading and hope I find something sooner rather than later."

I placed a hand on his back and looked at his red eyes and the dark circles under them. He was working himself into the ground and had been doing so for more than a few days now.

"Jeez, Caleb. When was the last time you slept?" I asked him.

Annabel put Nora down in her crib and turned to us again.

"Probably five days ago. He keeps taking that caffeine boost spell he sells at his shop to keep him going. All he does is read," she said.

"Baby, you have to slow down," I said.

Caleb shook his head as if I'd suggested he give up his firstborn to the devil.

"No. What if I stop and he comes after you next, or Ann, or Nora, or anyone else? I can't lose you guys. I won't let him take you away from me. Not again."

Annabel and I exchanged a look and she bit her lip. I shrugged.

"I'm going to regret this," Annabel said, taking her shoes off. "Babysitting is over. You're off tonight."

"What? What are you talking about? You're going out with your girlfriends," Caleb said.

"No. Not anymore. You're going out with your *somewhat* handsome boyfriend and giving yourself a night off and a good night's sleep, or banging," Annabel said, and I looked up at her.

The nod she gave me was barely noticeable, but I got the message. "You're welcome," it said.

"No, no, Annabel. It's fine. I'll stay in and watch Nora," Caleb insisted.

Annabel came over to us and closed the book Caleb had been reading and then took it in her arms and held it there, out of Caleb's reach.

"If you stay in, you'll give yourself another dose of that wretched spell, and you'll keep reading. Gee, Caleb, I love reading as much as any other girl, but you're taking this to a whole other level. Take the night off. Go have dinner somewhere poncy or something. Have some fun. Then come back here tomorrow and get back to work. You deserve it. Both of you do."

Before Caleb could protest again, I dragged my hand down to the small of his back and gave him a kiss on the neck.

"Listen to Annabel, baby. She's right," I whispered in his ear. "Come on. Let's go out and grab some dinner."

I felt Caleb melt under my touch, and I knew I had him now. I helped him get up and followed him to his bedroom. Before he closed the door, he stood to the side and turned to Annabel.

"I hate you, bossy lady," he told her and grabbed the door handle.

"Love you too, asshole." She chuckled just as the door shut, and we were left on our own.

"Do we have to go?" he cried. "Do you want me to take some reading material with us?"

I shook my head and took his hands.

"No reading allowed. Get dressed. I'm going to take you somewhere nice," I said and led him to his wardrobe.

Once he'd got dressed and splashed some cold water on his face, we were on our way to the city center.

I'd never ventured much into Soho, especially not anywhere past Chinatown, but I knew there were lots of gay bars in the area where we could escape from the Nightcrawler witch world and feel normal for a while without being stared at, whether because of our witch and hunter relationship or because of our sexuality.

I took us into a gay pub and ordered us two pints of lager while I got Caleb to loosen up and put Christian to the back of his mind.

"I was talking to Winston earlier," I said.

"Wow. Well done. Great accomplishment."

I could see he was still mulling over all the crap he'd been reading before we'd left the house. But I wasn't going to give up so easily.

If I knew one thing, it was what Caleb really liked more than anything.

"He mentioned douching. Do you know what that is?"

As expected, his eyes darted to mine, and the expressionless face turned into a curious one.

"Of course I do. But why were you two talking about douching?"

"Well..." I started and looked at the other patrons around us. No one seemed to be paying us much attention, although I did get a couple of mischievous smiles from guys dressed in leather. "He was saying how he and Hew have tried, you know, bottoming, and he was shocked I hadn't."

Caleb choked on his beer, and I patted his back to help the liquid go down the right hole.

"Well, would that interest you?" he asked when he managed to find his composure.

I shrugged. "Is it something that you want? I'd

never thought about it, but...if you'd like to fuck me..."

Caleb caressed my cheek and gave me a tender kiss on the lips, only when he pulled back, he bit down on my bottom lip and didn't let go until he saw me wince.

"I mean, sure, we can try. But I like—no, *love*—you fucking me," he slurred, and if my dick hadn't sprung to attention with the biting, it certainly did with the words that came out of his mouth.

"I love fucking you too," I whispered in his ear, and I heard a little whimper escape him.

He traced his hand down my chest, and just as he groped me, he stood up so he hid the move with his body, but that didn't stop a few whistles from some of the patrons.

"Baby, you better stop this unless you want me to come in my pants," I said in his ear.

"Do you promise?" he whispered back and bit my earlobe.

And we were officially in trouble. Which was good. At least I'd taken his mind off Christian. But now he had sex on his mind, and there was nothing we could do about it.

"Have you ever had sex in a public bathroom?" he mumbled.

His hand tightened around my cock, and I bit my lip to stop myself from growling.

"No, why—" I started saying, but before I could finish, he grabbed my hand and led me down the other side of the pub.

As I walked behind him, hand in hand, a guy slapped my butt, and when I gave him evil eyes, he licked his upper lip and winked at me.

"Lucky bastard," he said to me.

Fuck!

Was this really going to happen? In public? It wasn't that I'd never thought of it, but with a killer instinct, I'd preferred to keep it in the house where there had been plenty of ropes and cuffs to keep me from hurting people.

Caleb led the way down a narrow staircase and pushed the door with the male figurine on it. As we entered, I saw two guys standing at the urinals next to each other, their hands crossed over the other man's dick. They both turned to look at us, and they looked horny and high.

They continued to stare at us, palming each other's dicks as if we were their own personal porn channel, until Caleb locked us in the booth, and I turned my attention back to him.

Caleb pinned me against the wall and ground himself on me. His dick was as hard as mine, and I didn't need to take his pants off to see its shape as the skinny jeans he loved wearing did all the talking.

"You're killing me here," I told him when he came up for air from the juicy, wet kiss he gave me.

"But, baby, I'm just getting started," he said, and I felt a jolt of energy as he made our empathic connection work both ways and let me into his head.

This might be a bit more private, don't you think? Although I have to say, having spectators would make me hornier, he said in my head.

I bit my lip to keep me from moaning as he unzipped my trousers and took my length into his mouth hungrily.

His passion and horniness shot throughout my body like a lightning bolt that kept striking, as if on loop. It was a miracle I wasn't coming, but my body was getting accustomed to being in complete unison with his, so it took more than a simple touch to make me come.

Don't worry, baby. If you come, I can make you horny again, he said.

Jesus, what are you doing to me?

Of course, he was doing the best thing. Sucking me off like a champ. I'd never been blown like this from anyone before him. No woman had even come close to doing this so masterfully, so orgasmically as he did.

I would love to have said it was because he was a man and knew what was hot or not, but I had sucked him off enough times to know I didn't even come close to his artful blowjobs. But I was learning. Our empathic link allowed me to not only hear his thoughts but access what he wanted me to do and how he felt when I did it.

Don't sell yourself short. You're a pretty good blower. And an even better top, he said.

No, he wasn't just the best blowjob I'd had. He

was the best sex I'd ever had. Nothing even came close to what it felt like being with Caleb. Being inside Caleb.

He swallowed my length all the way and kept his nose to my groin while massaging the part of my shaft where it met my balls with his thumb and my taint with his index.

I felt as if someone had cut my oxygen tank, and I was struggling to breathe. It felt as if he was choking me, like we did at other times.

Before I could unwind, he came up for air, and I felt as if I could breathe again too. But only for a moment because he did the same thing.

I'm not going to last long, I told him.

Good. Come in my mouth, baby.

As he gave me permission, his middle finger tickled my anus and pressed against it, although he didn't insert his finger.

He might as well have because I clenched and felt my dick tremble.

Come on, he said and pushed against the side of my anus harder.

I held my breath and continued to resist his touch.

Why are you resisting me? he asked.

You have your fun; I have mine.

He choked as my glans rubbed on his pharynx, and I thought he would let me go again so he could catch some air.

Instead, he dug his finger into my hole, and I felt

the cum shooting out of me and down his throat before I could control it.

I let out a groan and a silver dust spilled from my mouth.

One moment we were both feeling my bliss, the next Caleb's entire body was encased in a slick cocoon, as if he'd been swallowed by an oversized condom, and he screeched.

His scream was loud and clear in my head.

What the fuck? I can't breathe!

I got down to my knees and touched Caleb everywhere, looking for the opening of the cocoon.

As with the vines, I couldn't find anything to break the spell. But I couldn't keep hoping the spell would expire. I had to do something before he suffocated inside the darn thing.

Help, he shrieked.

"I'm trying, baby, I'm trying."

I pulled at the latex over his mouth, hoping to make a tear in it, but this was no fucking latex, was it? This was something magical and impenetrable. What kind of kinky-ass spells had I sniffed to have all this weird-ass shit happen to us?

I needed to start carrying a knife with me. This was getting ridiculous.

"Hold on, baby."

Wade, I can't breathe. I'm gonna die.

Patting him down and pulling at the material

wasn't working. I needed to find something sharp right now.

I took a moment to look at my nakedness before I pulled up my trousers and rushed out of the door.

The two guys wanking each other off stared at me as I pulled the door open and ran upstairs. The bar was crammed with people waiting to order a drink.

I didn't have much time. I needed to get Caleb out of that fucking spell. A couple of guys with empty, tall glasses stared at me with a naughty grin.

I grabbed one of the glasses and smashed it on the table. A piece of glass dug into my palm, but I didn't have time to feel sorry for myself. I picked up a big chunk and returned downstairs.

It all happened in a flash. Seconds later, I was back at the stall with the two guys standing over Caleb, trying to get him out of the cocoon to no avail.

I pushed them aside and pressed the glass over his open mouth.

Relief washed over me as the glass cut through, and Caleb took a big gasp of air. I peeled the rest of it off him and uncovered his face.

"The fuck was that, dude? You a murderer?" one of the guys said.

"Was," I muttered and held Caleb in my arms.

I'm sorry. I'm so sorry. I'm a monster.

You are not, he said, but I had a hard time believing him after almost losing him.

NINE
CALEB

I still couldn't believe how close I'd come to dying. Again.

If Wade hadn't acted as fast as he had, I'd have suffocated inside the ectoplasm that had encased me.

It was simply incomprehensible how and why the spells he'd used in the past were coming back to haunt him. It seemed to happen every time he felt a strong emotional pull. The problem was, he wasn't a witch, so it shouldn't have mattered anyway. Besides, the last of those spells had been ground and inhaled a month ago. Surely his body would have flushed the dust residue out of his system by now.

"Caleb, I'm so sorry. I don't know what to say," he said for the hundredth time on the way back.

"Baby, if you tell me how sorry you are one more time, I'm gonna punch you so hard that you're not even going to enjoy it," I said to him and grazed his hand, giving him a full blast of my forgiveness, hoping it would help him get the message.

I wasn't angry with him. I was angry with myself because I'd thought it was a one-time occurrence, and I'd been too busy to give Wade's problem a second thought.

If there was anyone to blame about what had happened at the bathroom stall, that was me.

We didn't even manage to reach Covent Garden before my phone rang in an ominous way.

I didn't know how a mobile phone could sound ominous, especially since it didn't have a soul, but somehow, even before I answered it, I knew it was bad news.

"Hello," I said when the device touched my ear.

"Caleb," Lorelai cried. "You need to get here."

"El, what's going on? What happened?" I yelled, and some passers-by turned to stare me down. "Come where? The café?"

"I'll text you the address. You-you better hurry. This is ugly," she said and hung up before I could get anything else out of her.

The phone immediately lit up in receipt of her much-promised message.

"Is she okay?" Wade asked.

"I don't know. She didn't say. She just said it's ugly and that I needed to get there fast."

"Get where?"

"Greek Street," I said and turned on my heel.

"That's back in Soho. Do you think she knows what I did?" he asked and hurried as I sprinted back in the direction we'd come from.

"How could she? The only ones who saw me were two drunk, horny idiots who probably don't even remember any of it."

It didn't take us long to get back to Cambridge Circus in Soho, and when we did, we saw the blue flashing of police cars and the fluorescent color of an armada of ambulances.

"This isn't good," I muttered.

"No, it doesn't look good," he said, and we pushed through the people watching the police cars, trying to understand what was going on.

We tried going into Moor Street when two police officers stopped us.

"I'm sorry, folks, road is closed," the female officer said.

"What happened?" Wade asked just as I said, "I'm with them."

"I'm afraid I can't divulge any information," the officer said but stopped mid-sentence when I pointed at a group of three people dressed in suits and talking to a constable.

"You're with the special unit?" she said and perked her eyebrow to look me up and down.

I nodded.

"Wait here," she said and walked a couple of steps

before shouting, "Hey, Tony. This guy's saying he's with them."

"Who are they?" Wade whispered.

"Witches undercover in MI5," I replied just as the officer returned her attention to me and pointed behind her with her thumb.

"You can go," she said and stepped aside to let us through.

I walked towards the three witches, trying desperately to remember their names and failing miserably, when one of them, the woman among them, stretched out her hand and shook mine. I pulled my glove down halfway to my palm so when she touched me, our skins met.

"Mr. Carlyle," she said.

Agent Adeyemi, she thought, and I picked up on it.

It was a natural instinct to want to introduce yourself when you shook someone's hand. And that's all I needed to jolt my memory.

"Corrine," I said. "Good to see you again. Long time no see."

"I wish our reunion was under better circumstances," she said. "You remember agents Harrison and Travis."

"Of course. Maximilian. Dirk," I replied, taking their hands one at a time.

"I don't believe I've met you before," Corrine said, looking at Wade.

Wade nodded and shook her hand.

"Wade. Nice to meet you."

"Are you new to the coven?" she asked.

"Couldn't be newer. Literally, just joined." I replied for him. "What happened here?"

Corrine started walking towards Greek Street, and we followed behind her.

"We've never seen anything like this before. It's unprecedented. We've had to take over and claim it was a gas leak, but—" Corrine said, but once we turned the corner, I saw the bright red hair of Lorelai hunched over a lamppost, puking up her guts, and I ran over to her.

"El, you okay? What happened?" I asked her and massaged her back as soon as I reached her.

Her eyes were red and her eyelids wet. She gave Wade a once over and then turned to me.

"It's horrible, Caleb. I can't believe anyone would do this," she said, and the tears rolled again.

"Do what?" I asked.

I was starting to lose my patience. Everyone was on edge and speaking in riddles as if we were on a fucking film and we needed to build up suspense or something. She'd called me here, so she'd better tell me what happened before I blew off.

"I can't even bring myself to say it," she said and stood up straight and gave a quick glance to her left at a black entrance with a neon sign that read Xtasy. Then, after a big breath, she walked over and the officer blocking the door opened it for us. Another one handed us gloves and we were swallowed up in the darkness of a foyer area. Our eyes took a couple of seconds to adjust and then we descended the stairs.

Once we reached the bottom, I saw teams of crime scene investigators and emergency services covering bodies with sheets.

The lights were up in the main bar. It was a tiny club, and I'd been here in my youth but never really visited since then. It was known as a den for the queer community and those looking to escape reality. Over the years, it had become a Nightcrawler haunt too. Lots of LGBTQ familiars had found their mate in here.

Despite its size, it looked like a stadium, the floor covered with white sheets wherever I looked. There were glasses and bottles on every table, on the bar top, and on the limited seating. But no one was nursing those drinks. The ice cubes had melted, and the drinks left wet rings on the wooden tables.

"What the...fuck?" I said.

"Oh God," Wade said at the same time.

"Over a hundred victims. All dead," Lorelai said, her voice barely a whisper.

"H-how?" I asked.

"We-we don't know. The coroner said they are not showing any signs of foul play. It looks like their hearts just...stopped. But he'll know more once he's examined them all."

"Their…what?" Wade shouted, and the few investigators turned to look at him.

"A group of friends called the police when they entered the club and saw all of them on the floor," she said.

"Caleb." I heard Graham behind us. "You came."

I didn't even have the energy to tell him I hadn't come for him.

"Graham, who did this?" I asked.

"We don't know. I've tried a variety of spells, but they're not giving me anything."

"It's Christian, isn't it?" Wade heaved.

We all turned to him and saw his face turn red. He looked as if he was about to explode. I recognized the look. The same look he'd had when he'd tried to kill me the first time he'd met me a month ago.

I touched his arm, but it didn't even register with him. If his outbursts were linked to his emotions, like a witch's powers were linked to their emotions, this could be the start of another episode. And we were already in the shit. We couldn't risk getting into more trouble. Especially considering the fact we couldn't know which spell would manifest.

"Baby, calm down. Please," I said, but it was too late.

The last thing I remember was Wade coughing purple dust. Then everything else became a blur.

———

When I opened my eyes, one thing became clear to me. I was no longer at the club, and my body felt like lead.

I could hear commotion around me, but I couldn't turn my head to find the source. All I could do was scan with my eyes and hope to get a clue of where the hell I was.

The ceiling was light blue, and I could see a railing at the edge of my vision with a red curtain. Neither my house nor Wade's had a blue ceiling or red curtains.

I squeezed my eyes shut and tried to realign with my body. I moved my toes, and they obeyed me. Then I tried my fingers and they curled into fists. My limbs were responsive, so why wasn't my head.

"Caleb." I heard Wade's voice, and he leaned over me, his blue eyes sparkling in the artificial light of the room. "Are you okay?"

As if his words were a spell, my body jolted into action, and I was finally able to move my head. I sat up. That was a mistake. The whole room turned, and I had to steady myself on Wade even though we weren't really moving.

"What...what happened?" I asked and blinked, clearing my vision and making everything stop jumping.

It appeared we were in a function room, and I'd been lying on the floor, which was carpeted with a crimson red pattern that had only been in style two hundred years ago. There were a few tables dotted around and fixed seating against one wall where Lorelai and Graham were being tended to by Corrine and Maximilian.

"I-it happened again, Caleb. A spell came out of me and put you all to sleep. I couldn't control..." He panicked, and if there was any doubt before, there was none now.

His outbursts were linked to his emotions, and God knew what could happen if he had another episode right now.

"Wade, look at me," I said and touched his chest.

He didn't.

I took my glove off and touched him again. This time he had no choice but to obey.

"This is not your fault. It was a mistake, okay? You didn't mean it."

"I just became so...so angry and upset, I..." He was getting wound up again, so I pushed happy thoughts on him.

"What the hell?" Graham shouted, turning all in the room to his direction.

"Mr. Durham, I'm glad to see you're okay," Corrine told Graham as he sat up.

"What happened?" he asked.

"It seems that Mr. Rawthorne lost control of his power when he saw the scene at Xtasy."

Graham's gaze fell on Wade.

"You? You're not witch," he shouted.

I looked at Wade, and he looked at me, biting his lip.

What did you do? I asked him.

I had to say something. Sorry, it was the only thing I could think of.

"He isn't? He told us he had the ability to put people to sleep—" Corrine started, but she stopped when Graham jumped out of his seat and barreled towards us.

Lorelai also stood and watched the events unfold.

"What the hell did you do to us? Why are you lying?" He grabbed Wade by the collar, and I had to intervene before they both did something they were going to regret.

"Graham, stop. It's not his fault, okay? He can't control it," I said.

"Can't control what?"

"He gets these outbursts in the last few days. When he gets too emotional—"

"What outbursts? He is not a witch. I could feel it if he was."

"I'm not. It's the spells," Wade said, and Graham tightened his grip.

"What spells?" he shouted.

I put my hand on Graham and forced him to calm down.

"He used to do spells, okay? When he was under Christian's rule, Christian made him think he was addicted to spell powder, and he would steal it from his victims and sniff it. And now, for some reason, because of the ley lines, they're all coming out at the worst of times," I said, and Graham took a step back, pushing my hand away from him.

"That's why you came to me," he mumbled.

Wade nodded.

"Wait a sec. You went to him? When? Why didn't you tell me?"

Since when did Wade seek help from my high priest? And why wouldn't he tell me?

Because I'd stop him. That's why. I would never want him to go to Graham for help after what he'd done, and Wade was desperate.

"Why didn't you say so? We could have gone to her again for help. Together," I said.

Wade turned and his eyelids dropped in defeat.

"She can't help."

"Who are you talking about?" Graham asked.

"And what did he do for you?" I asked, ignoring Graham.

"He gave me"—Wade put his hand in his pocket and pulled a stone out—"this."

"You haven't used it yet?" Graham asked. Wade shook his head. "What the hell are you waiting for?"

"Well, I can't exactly activate it myself, can I? I'm not a witch."

"What is it?" I asked.

Wade looked at me apologetically.

"It's a magic dampener," Graham said. "I use it for new witches until they can learn to tame their powers."

"I'm so confused," Maximilian said.

"Give it here. I'll activate it," Graham said and tried to take the stone from him, but Wade closed his fist before he got to it.

"I'd rather it was Caleb," he said and turned to me. "I'm sorry I didn't tell you. I wanted to make things better and give you one less thing to worry about. I was going to ask Hew to cast it on me, but then I didn't have an episode in a week, so I thought it was all over. I should have known it wouldn't be."

I touched the hand holding the spell and decided to give some privacy to this conversation.

I don't care that you didn't tell me. I'm just confused why you didn't let me help you.

You've got enough on your plate as it is.

And I'm happy to carry your problems, too, instead of having to find out like this when it's too late to do anything.

"Are they, like, having a moment, or have I gone deaf?" Maximilian said, and I shot him some evil glares.

"Okay, let's do this then," I said and placed my palm over his, covering the spell. "The spellword?"

"Protect," both Graham and Wade said at the same time.

I barely had time to open my mouth before the spell sparked to life, and the dust sparkled as Wade's body absorbed it. That hadn't happened before. Was it Graham's speaking that managed to activate it or were my spell casting powers growing stronger?

"How will we know it worked?" Wade asked.

"It has," Graham said.

We just wait and see, I guess.

"And if it hasn't, we'll put you under quarantine until it's all flushed out of your system," Graham added.

"No one is going in quarantine," I said.

Lorelai stepped into the middle and lifted her phone.

"You guys," she said, and at that moment Corrine's, Maximilian's, and Dirk's phones all broke into song at the same time.

"This doesn't sound good," Wade said.

"It isn't," Lorelai said and grabbed the remote on top of the bar and turned the TV on.

The screen filled with shots of the Thames and flashing blue lights. If I hadn't read the news headline underneath the reporter, it could have looked like a celebratory newsfeed of New Year's Eve and the fireworks at midnight.

Lorelai cranked the volume up, and the reporter's voice filled the room.

"Waves never seen before on the Thames hit the shores at Westminster. The metropolitan police commissioner has stated that at this point, the number is likely to be in the dozens if not hundreds—"

Lorelai hit the mute button as all the agents took their respective calls.

"What the fuck is happening?" I said. "This can't

be Christian. He couldn't possibly cause this much destruction."

"No," Graham agreed. "This can't be him. He's not a witch, and this is the work of witches."

"Who would do this? The high council?" I said. But why would they hurt humans?

"The high council would never do anything like this. It must be the new witches that went underground." Graham growled.

This wasn't possible.

"Okay, let's say you're right. How on earth have four-week-old witches mastered their powers to such an extent to cause this?" I asked.

"We'll have to go and find out," Wade said. "We've got to help these people. Whoever is causing this is not human, and the human authorities need our help."

Wade was right. The three MI5 agents might be powerful witches, but they weren't enough to help with a public magical attack of this level. We had to do something. Before more people got hurt.

TEN

WADE

Corrine led all of us downstairs and towards the cars parked in the middle of the street. Graham got in her car with Dirk, and Caleb followed Maximilian, only Graham stopped him.

"Caleb, I want you in the car with me."

"You don't tell me what to do, old man," Caleb said and Graham flinched.

If that picture I'd seen on his mantelpiece was any indication, he truly cared about Caleb and wanted to protect him, which I could appreciate. Even if he was trying to protect him from me. He needed it. And so did everyone else.

"I need to talk to you, and I won't take no for an answer," he insisted.

Caleb turned to me and I gave him the go-ahead. He responded with his eyes, and I didn't need to touch him to know he was saying he was here for me.

"Lorelai, you go with Maximilian," Graham said.

"Are you out of your mind? I'm not going in a car with a ticking time bomb," she shrieked and got in Corrine's car.

Caleb mouthed an "I'm sorry" before ducking inside the car and leaving me on the street with Maximilian.

He wasn't a bad-looking fellow. He had blond, short hair and striking green eyes. Maximilian looked like a guy who worked out, a lot, and if he was part of MI5, I couldn't blame him. He probably had to deal with bullshit like this more often than not.

"You don't have to put me in your car if you don't want to." I decided to make his decision easier as he walked over to the driver's side. It was still to be determined whether Graham's spell had worked on me and I didn't want anyone feeling on edge because of me.

Maximilian looked up at me and grinned.

"I've had actual bombs tied on me. I think I'll be fine," he said and got in the car.

He was already growing on me. I joined him in the car, and he sped off almost as soon as my door shut.

"Have you been a witch for long?" I asked him.

"Longer than I care for," he said. "You? Been a witch hunter for long?"

I wasn't sure how he knew. No one had mentioned it when we were in the room, and I'd made sure not to show any signs that I'd once been one. But I guess the resentment Graham showed me, paired with the stuff mentioned about Christian, might have given it away.

"Longer than I care for," I offered back.

"What brought you to the right side?"

"Caleb."

Maximilian smirked.

"Of course. Caleb is one hell of a guy. I'm not surprised."

I couldn't help wondering if he knew from personal experience, and I didn't know if I wanted the answer.

"I never slept with him, if that's what you're wondering. But I know people who have."

The look I gave him must have been scary because he quickly backtracked.

"Okay, okay. Not people. Person. One. A cyclops."

Caleb had mentioned a cyclops in his life, but he'd chosen not to say much about him, just enough for me to know he'd met him shortly after losing me and his memories.

"So, you're friends with Caleb's ex?"

Maximilian didn't answer straight away. There was more to the story, and I knew it.

"Well, he's my boyfriend," Maximilian said.

"Oh." It came out of me before I could stop myself. There was definitely a story there. But now was probably not the right time to find out.

"Oh, indeed."

He drove us through the busy streets of London,

rushing past traffic with the blue lights and siren his car came with, following Corrine's right in front of us.

"I can't believe you're a witch and you work in MI5. Witch hunter me would be livid," I said to him.

"Why? We've got to take positions within the government, otherwise our secrets and our world can be exposed."

"It makes sense. But that's not why. It's because Christian had us convinced *we* were a secret branch of the government."

"Maybe it wasn't all lies."

"What do you mean?"

"We take positions in secret. That doesn't mean the government hasn't created a secret branch to battle the paranormal. If there's one thing you should know about the Nightcrawler world, it's that nothing is black and white."

I nodded.

"I actually know that very well."

We didn't get a chance to say anything else before Maximilian came to a stop in front of the Westminster Bridge. The commotion of EMTs was overwhelming, and when we stepped out of the car, we had to tread carefully as there were people being resuscitated or tended to everywhere.

As with the scene at the club, there were lots of white sheets around, too, and the media was desperate to get snaps of the disaster.

Oh, the joys of the press. No respect for the victims

or those hard at work to save as many lives as they could.

We joined Caleb and the rest of them and passed the crime scene police tape that was stopping bystanders from getting any closer.

I touched Caleb's wrist as we walked and checked on him.

Did he piss you off? I asked him.

When does he not?

He asked about my outbursts, didn't he?

Uhm, no. He was trying to find out who the witch was that you went to for help.

Of all the things I'd expected Graham to concentrate on, Mother Red Cap was not one of them.

You didn't tell him about her, did you?

Are you crazy? I don't want to suffer for the rest of my life for revealing her secret.

Once we got to the edge of the river, the witches got to work inspecting every surface, looking for dust residue and casting spells to find out more about what had led to the waves.

Instead of adding nothing to their research, I decided to help a first responder who was trying to resuscitate a young woman.

"What happened?" I asked the nurse, who looked at me, panting and shaking.

This wasn't good. If she couldn't keep her shaking under control, she couldn't keep her strength in check either, and she could end up cracking the poor woman's ribcage.

"She went into cardiac arrest. I don't know what happened.".

I tried to take over from her, but she wouldn't move.

"I'm trained in first aid. I can help. If you don't let me, you're going to break her ribs," I yelled, and she hesitantly let go and let me take over.

"Get the oxygen mask," I said to her, calmly this time.

The nurse looked around her on the verge of tears, and I knew I had to keep her under control if we were going to save the woman.

"Look at me. What's your name?"

"Maria." She trembled.

"Maria, I need you to do one thing and one thing only. See that ambulance right there." I glanced behind her and she followed my gaze. Maria nodded. "I need you to run there and grab an oxygen mask. Can you do that?"

Maria nodded again.

"Go, now," I said, and she stumbled to her feet and raced across the pavement to the ambulance.

"Hold on, sweetheart. Hold on," I begged the young woman whose life was quite literally in my hands.

I looked up to check on Maria's progress, and I spotted a group of people in the distance that didn't seem to be involved in any of the rescue mission. It was dark and the light was limited on them, but all I could tell was that there were four of them, and they were all huddled together, watching the events unfold.

Maria returned with the oxygen mask, and I barely registered her as she unwound the tube and placed the mask on the victim's face.

"I'm so sorry. I'm new. This is literally my first shift, and we were all called out to help," she said.

I only looked at her for a second to reassure her it was okay, and by the time I turned my head back at the gang, they were gone.

The woman's heartbeat pulsed in my hands, and when I looked down at her, she was taking on the oxygen and breathing.

"Maria, are you all right to take over?"

"Yes, thank you. Thank you so much. You saved my life. And hers."

I acknowledged her gratitude with a nod, and I ran towards the spot I'd seen the gang. What was it they said about the suspect returning to the scene of the crime? Maybe they'd never left. Maybe they'd stuck behind to make sure the chaos they'd caused lasted long enough.

I didn't know what it was, but I was willing to find out. When I reached the spot, I peered behind me. There was a perfectly clear view of the entire bankside. I even spotted a certain silver-haired beaut hard at work.

This was getting weirder and weirder. Was I right? Had that group been responsible for what happened here?

I walked farther into the alley that the group must have disappeared into, but there was no one there.

I reached a crossing and turned left, too late to realize this was a setup.

And it was, because as soon as I took the turn, a man appeared behind me while another two men and a woman stood in front of me, full of smug faces and stupid grins.

"Who are you?" I shouted.

I was hoping my voice carried down to the riverside, but I wasn't holding any hope of being saved. As far as I knew, I was on my own.

"We are the second coming," the woman hissed.

"We are the new age," the man behind me said.

"You are psychos," I hissed in the same manner they did. "What do you want? Why are you doing this?"

"To end the human race," one of the men in front of me called out, and a gust of wind knocked me off my feet and carried me across the street.

Before I collapsed on the guy that had appeared behind me, he raised his hand, and I felt whiplash as I flew back towards the three witches. This time I came down to the ground, hard, my arm making a cracking sound and pain shooting through me with all its might.

When I growled, I made sure to do so as loud as I could. I might have been on my own, but I still held out hope that my voice would carry down and that Caleb would notice I was gone.

The female witch stepped closer to me and kicked my other arm, the one I hadn't just broken.

Her eyes glistened as she made a fist with her hand, and before I had the time to do anything, whether shout for help, cry, or duck to the side, the air left my lungs, and I was struggling to breathe.

I rolled away from her foot with my broken arm and all—and it was definitely broken because not only did it hurt like a mother, but it was also limp and lifeless next to me—and made my entire body convulse with pain.

I opened my mouth to scream, but instead, dust came out. The dust splattered over me and gave me my breath back. Before any of the witches could react, I coughed another ball of dust, and it floated above us all.

The dust was dark and ominous, and it took shape within moments, moments the witches didn't have to contemplate their next move. Spears made of shadows shot out in all directions. Countless numbers of them. I felt like I was suddenly in a medieval war film, and I was in the middle of the battlefield.

One by one, the witches got speared and collapsed in heaps on the ground without so much as a cry for help. Their blood painted the cobbled street red, and as if it was all a dream, the dust spears evaporated, leaving no trace of foul play behind them. Other than four dead bodies, of course.

I stumbled to my feet and ignored the pain in my arm as I pounded down the alley to the riverside where Caleb was.

I didn't realize he was talking to Winston until I was standing in front of them and looking into their faces. Both were white as if they'd seen a ghost.

"What?" I asked them, and Caleb noticed my arm.

"Are you okay? Where did you get that souvenir?" he asked looking at my face, but the snark and worry were missing from his voice.

I turned to Winston who looked equally terrified.

"Win, what's going on? Why do you look like you two got the worst paycheck in the history of paychecks?"

"Wade," Caleb said. "It's Hew. Someone has taken him. He's missing."

Eleven

Caleb

Three massive terror attacks were bad enough, but Hew being abducted? That shit was becoming personal, and I wasn't having any of it.

I couldn't even begin to imagine what Winston felt like, losing his mate in that manner with no explanation as to what was happening and no way he could stop it.

There was not much consolation for a guy who had lost everything once before.

"The worst part is I can't feel him," he said.

"What do you mean you can't feel him?" I asked.

We'd retreated from the Thames shores and to an ambulance where we could sit him down.

"Since...since we bonded, I could feel him. It's like a radar inside my head that can sense him and that gets hotter and louder the closer I get to him."

I didn't imagine it was easy to describe what it felt like being mated with someone. But he was doing a damn good job.

"Since he was abducted, I can't feel him. It's like someone's cut our bond, but I know that's impossible."

Wade gazed at me, and so did Winston, expectantly, as if I had the answer to everything and the magical fix-it-all. I wish I did, but I was far from the powerful witch they thought I was.

"What happened? How do you know he was abducted?" I asked.

Winston took a deep breath as he relived the events of his lover's disappearance, and I tried to pick up any details he might have thought irrelevant.

"We were supposed to go and offer our services to the Crow. He's friends with the owner, and he wanted us to convince the guy that I could work security some nights to help keep everyone safe. You know, build the trust and everything.

"We were meeting outside the pub so we could go in together. He was already waiting when I got there, and all I had to do was wait for the traffic lights and cross the street. But I didn't get a chance.

"A black SUV appeared out of nowhere and stopped in front of the Crow. When it was gone, so was Hew," Winston said. "I tried to follow them, but the van was going at a crazy speed, and I lost them. I was going to use my connection with him to keep hot on their tail, but as I was running and getting closer, I lost him. As if he..."

Winston closed his eyes and bit down whatever thought was gnawing its teeth in his head. It wasn't difficult to guess. If the familiar bond was impossible to sever, then it was entirely possible Hew was...

No, he couldn't be. The death of a mate was felt. I'd heard of way too many widowed witches succumbing to depression and oblivion after the loss of their mate.

Hew was still alive. I was sure of that. But something seriously dangerous was at play here.

"I think it's time for the big guns," I said, and both brothers lifted their gazes to meet mine.

"What do you mean?" Winston asked.

Instead of answering, I turned and scanned the crowd of EMTs, police officers, and field agents looking for the familiar face of my high priest.

"I'll be right back," I told them and gave Wade a gentle squeeze of the hand to reassure him, but he winced in pain.

"What's wrong with your hand?" I asked him.

Wade looked from me to his brother and then back to me before he spoke.

"I broke it."

"What? How?"

I'd only left him on his own for five minutes. What the hell did he get up to, to end up with a broken arm?

"I got ambushed by some witches," he said and

explained what happened at the alley. "I'm fine now. Go speak to Graham. It's okay."

I shook my head and wrapped my fingers around his arm.

"Not before I've fixed you," I said and used another healing crystal on him.

If we kept ending up in trouble like this, I might have to mortgage our house to afford the healing spells we were going through.

Once I'd made sure he was fine and Winston was sort of okay, I left them to their own devices and approached Graham, who was analyzing some dust residue, and interrupted his concentration.

He turned to look at me, questions in his eyes.

"Did you find something?" he asked.

I shook my head. "It's time you for you to help, though."

"What does it look like I'm doing?" He chuckled and tried to return to the residue.

"For years, I've watched the high council give out orders and sit back while everything fell into place around them. Whenever something big happens, they take credit while the coven does all the hard work. And when things fail, it's always the witches under their servitude who take the fall."

"That's what the high council is there for, Caleb-boy. They make the hard decisions and make sure we are safe."

"Are you seriously still taking their side after what

they made you do? No! That's not what the high council is. They don't work hard. We are the ones working hard to keep us and them safe. But it's time they played their part."

"What do you mean?" Graham asked.

"They are some of the strongest witches, aren't they? It's time they showed us their strength and help us stop Christian and the witches who are out of control. You need to set up a meeting."

Graham shook his head with uncertainty.

"I don't think that would be a good idea, Caleb. You're not in their good books."

"Good. They're not in my good books, either. We've got something in common. Set up a meeting. Now," I yelled and made sure he got the message. If he didn't do what I told him, there would be consequences. High priest or not, I'd make him pay.

Graham fidgeted as he tried to get his phone out of the pocket of his jacket, and he flipped the antique phone, which he considered more secure, open.

As soon as the device touched his ear, he spoke on it.

"We need to talk. Things are getting serious," Graham said.

"I'll say." I huffed, and Graham reached up to block the microphone with his hand and gave me an evil glare.

"When?" he said. I pointed my finger at the ground, and he said, "Now."

Then, as quickly as he'd made the call, he ended it and slipped his phone back into his pocket.

"And?"

"Let's go," he said, giving up on trying to convince me otherwise.

I glanced at the ambulance and whistled. Both Winston and Wade looked at me and stood as soon as I called them.

"No, no, no, Caleb. You can't bring witch hunters to the council. They will punish you. They will punish all of us," Graham shrieked.

"Non. Negotiable," I said to him very slowly so that he got every part and understood the meaning.

"Where are we going?" Lorelai asked as she joined us and once both Rawthorne brothers were next to me.

"It's time I introduced Wade and Winston to the high council," I said.

Graham's despair showed on his face, and I couldn't help but be amused by it.

———

Even though he tried not to show it, I could tell Wade was nervous about meeting with the high council. He kept biting his lip and taking deep breaths.

I couldn't blame him. After all, they'd played such a big part in his career, even if they'd kept behind the scenes, and he owed them a lot of his guilt and shame.

Graham, Lorelai, and the three of us left the crime scene at the riverside behind us and headed for the City of London on foot.

As expected, Graham tried to change my mind about the brothers, but all I kept telling him was how non-negotiable it was. It was actually starting to irritate me. Graham had tried to convince me of how sorry he was for what he'd consented to do for them and for Christian, yet every step of the way he was only proving to me where his true loyalties lay.

Once upon a time, I'd considered this man the closest thing to a father that I'd ever had, yet with every word, every action, he was pushing me farther and farther away from him, and I couldn't make up my mind if I was more upset about what he'd done or about the death of our relationship.

"What can the high council do anyway?" Graham said as we approached London Bridge.

"It's time they stopped being the puppeteers and got their asses into action," I said. "They're powerful witches. The least they can do is help out the victims at the river or the investigation at Xtasy. Although, I'd much rather they put their powers and connections to good use and found the witches that are causing these disasters."

"Hear, hear," Lorelai added.

"They won't. They've sworn to stay out of the field. It's the only way to stay neutr—"

"Neutral? Really? Was it neutral sacrificing young

witches to Christian? It's not time to be neutral, Graham. It's time to act. Before a war breaks out and they are forced to take a side that's only going to make things worse," I shouted.

A group of friends boozing in the beer garden of a pub all stared at me with terror written in their faces.

We stopped in front of The Shard, London's tallest high-rise, which took its name from its shape. Four sides meeting at the top like shards of glass.

Graham looked up.

"What?" I asked.

"We're here."

"What do you mean here? Like, here, here?" I said, pointing at the skyscraper.

Graham nodded and headed for the entrance.

"You can't tell me the high council is based in a fucking skyscraper. That's ridiculous," I said, but Graham didn't seem to hear me anymore.

He approached the front desk and placed his arm on the surface, leaning casually on it.

"Here for H.C. Ward. Name is Durham. They're expecting us," he said.

The man at the desk typed something on his keyboard and nodded in approval.

"Please use lift number thirteen, Mr. Durham," he said and pointed to the lifts.

As soon as we approached number thirteen, the doors slid open and we all entered before the doors shut, and we were hoisted up into the skies.

I would never have thought the governing body of the coven would be based in the city. I'd always expected them to be tucked away underground in the catacombs of old London, sitting on thrones made of gold and velvet.

I expected the lift to stop on the second or third floor, or even the tenth, but instead, it kept going. It went past the twenties, the thirties, and even the forties. We eventually came to a stop on the sixty-sixth floor, and when the doors opened, I was the first to step out.

There were witch security guards every few feet, all holding staffs that were decorated with intricate spells that I could sense even from afar how strong they were.

They all inspected us as we walked past them. The walls behind them were decorated with famous paintings from across the ages. I noticed some Dalis, some Picassos, and some William Blakes among others I wasn't familiar with. Something told me, however, considering where we were and the security level, that those things weren't knock-offs.

"Where even are we?" Wade groaned.

"I know," I said as we followed Graham down corridors, which he was way too familiar with despite their intricacy.

"Nice to see how the other half lives, huh?" Lorelai said.

I didn't get the chance to agree with her or tell her if we kept the café that we'd be requesting a significant pay rise because Graham stopped in front of a white set of doors and knocked.

The knock sounded ominous, and I couldn't help feel a knot in the pit of my stomach. I was hoping I was doing the right thing. After everything that had happened, I shouldn't have come here, but I had to at least try, right?

We heard a loud unbolting sound and the door swung open slowly, letting us into a dimly lit board-room with the night skyline of London as the background.

People in suits were sat behind a long, u-shaped table, all looking serious and sinister.

"Graham," said a witch in the middle. I recognized her as high priestess Matilda, "You've...brought company."

She looked a lot different than when I'd met her before. While she'd been dressed casually when she'd introduced herself to me five years ago, she was now dressed to a T in a black trouser suit, her blonde hair stretched in a bun at the crown of her head.

Had she dressed down to meet me so she could appear friendly and down-to-earth, or was this her uniform?

"Caleb insisted," Graham said, and I could have punched him if I wasn't busy scanning the rest of the room, spotting more people I'd met over the years, all looking vastly different than they had before.

"Is it national suit day today? Did I miss the memo?" I asked.

No one seemed to respond to my joke, so I turned to Wade, but he was standing still, looking whiter than the wall behind him.

"We should have dressed up," I told Lorelai, and she nodded.

At least she wasn't terrified of facing the high council. That was some consolation.

"Yes, I've got a great red suit at home. If Graham had told us, I'd have popped that on."

"We are not here to discuss suits," Graham said with a bitterness in his voice.

"Of course not," I snapped back at him. "We're here to talk about important issues. So, I'll jump straight in, shall I?"

"What do you want, Caleb? Why are you even here?" Matilda asked, and gone was the friendliness she'd once had in her voice, replaced by a cold, calculating woman.

"I want you to act," I said, raising my voice to match hers.

"What Caleb means—" Graham chuckled awkwardly and stepped in front of me.

I put my hand on his forearm and shot him with his own fear.

"Never do that again. If I want to explain something, I'll explain it myself," I said, and he cowered in the corner so I could take control of this conversation.

"Well, you are here now. Speak, Mr. Carlyle. What do you want us to act on?" Matilda said.

I wasn't going to be intimidated by her. These people disgusted me. They didn't deserve my fear or respect.

"Don't you know already? Christian is back stronger than before, and as if that wasn't enough of a threat, witches are attacking humans in terrorist acts I've not seen the likes of ever before." She didn't seem to react to my words.

I scanned the room and right at the end, on the other side of where Graham was standing, I spotted Ash.

Ashton Beauchamp. The man I'd been hired to protect not too long ago and who had ended up in my bed instead. Or, me in his bed, to be more accurate. He might have been uptight about our relationship and wanting to keep it a secret, but he didn't strike me as a bad guy.

Sure, he was filthy rich and didn't want to recreate a gay, witch version of *Pretty Woman* by taking a work-ing-class, poor little witch, but he couldn't have known about the horrors the high council had committed. Did he? Had there been anyone on the board that was actually a good person who didn't think crossing the line between good and evil was necessary to protect the witch world?

"And what do you suggest we do?" Matilda said sharply.

"What do you mean what should you do?" Lorelai shouted and stepped in front of me. "Come out and help us find those fucking witches. Are you people out of your mind? You're sitting here like fucking investors when hundreds of people have lost their lives tonight alone!"

"Watch your language, Lorelai. You're walking on very thin ice," Matilda said.

At that, I laughed. I couldn't stop myself. It was all I could do to keep me from spitting in their faces.

"She is walking on thin ice?" I shouted.

"I think we've heard enough," Matilda said and stood up, pushing her chair back with a shrieking, hair-raising sound.

"You've not heard anything close to enough." I growled.

Matilda's eyes glowed as she slammed her hand on the trestle table.

"Your time is up, Caleb. You dare to bring witch hunters to our base after everything they've done, and you disrespect the entire council by shouting in our faces? No, we have heard more than enough. I'd suggest you leave now, before I decide you need to be punished for this insubordination."

"What the—"

"We gave you a job to do, and you have failed miserably. This is your mess. You created it by trotting across London with a witch hunter up your ass, trying to prove what exactly? Christian is at large because of you. The ley lines are surging because of you. Everything that is happening is because of the decisions you made on that rooftop a month ago. Why do you think we assigned the job to you? It's your fault, you fix it," she said, and by the time she finished, she had to catch her breath.

I admired her passion and rigor, but I loathed every single word that had come out of her mouth.

"Are you people for real?" Wade said. "You call yourselves a council, yet you throw a member of your coven in the water with a rock and you expect him to float?"

Matilda glanced at him with a sour face and raised her hand to stop him.

"The high council doesn't listen to witch hunters."

"Maybe they should," Lorelai shouted. "Because I'll tell you what, nothing you've said has made any sense since we stepped into this room."

"Lorelai, please. This doesn't concern you," a man to Matilda's right yelled.

Lorelai shot him an evil glare.

"If you're not going to hear from a familiar or a witch hunter, you will hear it from a fellow witch," I said. "Maybe it is my fault that the ley lines are surging and Christian is at large. After all, I did decide to let myself get killed to save someone else. But does the entire high council know about your deal with Christian?"

"What deal?" Ash asked, and I gave him half a

smile for giving me the sign I needed to know I was doing the right thing.

If Ash didn't know, then perhaps there were more people in the dark than I'd thought.

"Whatever deal the high council made is none of your business, Caleb," Matilda said.

"Oh, but it is," I said. "And you better shut up now. You've said your piece, it's time to say mine."

Matilda gasped and her eyes glowed even brighter. So much so that her hands caught fire.

"Matilda! Calm down," the guy who had shouted at Lorelai a few moments ago said.

She looked at him and took a few breaths, the flames dying down.

"Now that you've thrown your toys out of the pram, may I?" I asked, and she shook her head. I didn't care. "I'm sure a lot of you know the deal you struck with Christian when I failed to retrieve his crystal. Because you people were scared I'd fallen in love with that asshole, and you didn't know how to destroy him, so you decided to let me live without my memories of that year I went undercover and where I hid the crystal that bound his life. But you had to do something to save yourselves. Was it you, Matilda? Or was it someone else who went to Christian and offered him fledgling witches in exchange for your safety?"

"What do you mean, Caleb?" Ash pushed his chair back and came to stand in front of the boardroom.

"Graham was feeding Christian the names of new

witches the council deemed weak. They had a quota to fill, you see. So, for five years, they sacrificed hundreds of witches to feed that monster."

His frown deepened and his dark eyes flared with disbelief.

"Is this true?" he asked Matilda.

"Most of them didn't have much of a future," she said, and I felt a fire erupt inside of me.

"How dare you justify your actions. Even if they didn't go on to become high fucking priests and priestesses, they still deserved a future," I shouted.

"Wh-why? Why would you agree to this? Who else knows about this?" Ash asked and scanned the room.

No one reacted.

"Speak, people. Open your motherfucking mouths and speak." He shouted this time.

We didn't get a chance to find out if Ash's words would spring anyone into action because the doors behind us burst open, and in a blur of fire and wind, Christian walked in, followed by Hew and the witch that had betrayed us, Danielle, and another dozen or so people behind them.

"Hew!" Winston shouted as the entire high council knocked their chairs over and grabbed for the crystals on their spellbooks.

Hew giggled and brushed Christian's arm.

"Guess again," Hew said in a higher pitch than his usual voice.

"Council, at the ready," Matilda shouted, and everyone held their spells out.

"H-how did you get through," I asked, but then I noticed the bloodbath behind them as the flames went down.

The security guards, the witches who'd been trained rigorously to keep the high council protected, were all dead.

"What a welcome," Christian said, but his voice sounded deeper. Darker. "I'm only here to talk."

"Attack," Matilda shouted, and a pandemonium of words and spells and dust suffocated the room so terribly I could barely see what was happening in front of my nose.

I hyperventilated. My hands shook. I started to panic and tried to sense Wade's position when the dust cleared and Christian, Hew, and the rest revealed themselves unscathed.

Hew was leaning forward, his face red, blowing at the dust, creating a whirlwind that drove the substance at the walls, painting it momentarily like a canvas.

"Hew, what are you doing?" Winston cried. "Why are you working with him?"

"What the hell just happened?" Ash asked at the same time.

Hew stepped forward and grinned, extending his arm towards Winston.

"Oh, sweet darling, I'm not Hew. I'm Rhafnet."

"Rhafnet? The...the demon?" Ashton mumbled.

Hew gave him an evil glare, verifying that indeed, there was no Hew left in that body.

"The Goddess, dear child! Has no one taught you to respect your creators?" Hew hissed.

"What creators? Hew, what are you talking about?" Winston asked.

"Council at the ready," Matilda shouted again, and I wanted to tell her to shut up.

Christian did it before I got the chance.

"Do shut up, witch. I'm here to make you an offer."

"We are done making offers with you, Christian," she yelled.

Christian's face hardened, and Hew came to his side, caressing his arm. It looked so wrong. Everything about what was happening in front of our very eyes was wrong.

"He's not Christian, either." Hew giggled.

"Then who are you?" I asked him.

Christian's black eyes stared me down until his lips twitched to the side.

"I'm Ealistair, your father. The father of all of you."

"What's he talking about?" Wade whispered to me.

Danielle stepped forward and tutted.

"You people call yourselves witches and you don't know where you came from? Ealistair and Rhafnet created us all and gave us our powers. Kneel at their service or die," she shouted.

"That will be enough, Danielle," Christian said.

"Forgive her. She didn't mean that," Hew said. "She had other plans, you see, and she's still bitter about it."

Danielle glared at Hew, and I could tell she wanted to say something, but she held herself back.

Before she could retreat behind Christian and Hew, I grabbed her wrist and forced myself inside her head.

I was supposed to take on Rhafnet. Not that filthy half-breed. This was not part of the plan. When I told Christian about the ley lines, I was supposed to take on the spirit of Rhafnet.

Danielle's anger was burning hot inside her, and her thoughts were a jumble. She pulled her hand away from me, blasting me with some invisible force.

"Don't touch me, traitor."

"Can someone explain what the fuck is going on?" Lorelai shouted.

I took a step forward, towards Christian and Hew. Wade tried to grab my hand and stop me, but I wasn't scared of them.

"I'm not the traitor, she is." I pointed at Danielle. "She never wanted to help Christian in the first place. She was the one that told him about the ley lines, but she kept part of the truth from him, didn't you? He'd thought he would feed on the magic underneath and live forever, when in reality, he'd be releasing two demons. You were supposed to host Rhafnet, but it didn't work out, did it?"

"Damn it, Danielle," Christian spat. "I told you I needed a psychic to take on my wife's spirit."

"It's true. I can't just take on anyone's body," Hew said. "It helps that he's a raven too."

"So...so Hew is really gone?" Winston asked.

Hew shrugged.

"He's still here somewhere, but I've put him to sleep. It's my time now." He smiled.

"Why would you want to release demons into the world?" I asked Danielle.

Her posture changed and went from a furious madwoman back to the mischievous witch she was.

"Be—"she started, but Christian didn't let her finish.

"Enough. We are your creators and you have two choices. You can choose to fight on our side, which you should, or you can fight against us and die."

"Fight who?" I asked.

Hew tapped Christian's chest lightly and tiptoed around to me.

"Humans have been running this world for way too long, don't you think? We've been forced to hide our true selves or die at their hands. That's not why I birthed you, my children. That's not why we created you. We made you to be better. We made you to rule," Hew said.

"You're talking genocide," Ash muttered. "How can you?"

"We call it survival of the fittest," Christian said. "So, who's with us? Who's ready for the rise of the witches?"

Matilda stepped forward and the entire room watched her.

"Is it...is it really you?" she asked.

"My child, of course. Let me look at you," Christian said, and she lifted her eyes to stare at him. "You've got fire in you, like me. I could use you in my new world. Imagine not having to answer to the humans. Imagine the humans having to answer to us. We can be their masters like we were always meant to be. We can start with London and work our way around until humans are a thing of the past. Join us. Join me, and you will be rulers beside me."

A chill cooled my core. All this time we'd thought Christian was behind this, but it was something worse. It was demons with plans of grandeur. This wasn't going to end well.

Matilda bowed to Christian and stood in front of him.

"Who's next?"

I glared at Matilda, but her confidence was back.

"You're a traitor to your kind," I told her.

Hew shook his finger at me playfully, a sly smile on his lips.

"Whoever doesn't join us is a traitor to their kind. Don't get things mixed up."

I looked behind me at the rest of the room. No one was moving. Everyone was staring at the intruders but not taking any action.

"I guess we're all—" I turned to say to him when I heard witches behind me approach and say, "I'm on your side."

Only they weren't on my side. They were on Christian's. The man that had shouted at Lorelai walked behind Hew, as did the people that'd been sitting next to him.

Soon, it felt like the entire room had decided to be murderers. I looked at who was left.

Ash was still behind me as was Graham. Ash I could expect, but Graham. I'd have thought he'd follow his leaders blindly.

There were another five witches I barely knew who had taken a stance against genocide and mass destruction. It wasn't anywhere near enough to stop the demons.

"I guess we'll see you when we kill you." Christian smiled and lifted his arm in the air.

Flames erupted out of it and engulfed everyone that had taken to his lies. When the flames disappeared, everyone was gone.

"Fuckety, fuck, and holy fuckballs," Lorelai said.

She could say that again.

TWELVE
WADE

"Yes...don't tell me. I'll call you when it's safe," Caleb was saying over the phone, and I wanted to hold his hand and tell him everything was going to be okay, but I couldn't bring myself to lie to him, especially when I didn't believe it, either.

"What did Annabel say?" I asked once he'd hung up.

Caleb sighed.

"She's scared. She's going to hide with Nora."

"Who can blame her? Aren't we all?" Lorelai said.

"Is there anywhere safe for her to go?" I asked.

Was there any safe space when demons were out on the loose and determined to wreak havoc on the world as we knew it.

"Yes, she's got connections with other trolls, and if trolls are good at one thing, that's hiding," he said, but it didn't make me feel any less scared for her and baby Nora.

"How do we stop them? What could we possibly do to stop demons?" the man that had taken Caleb's side earlier asked.

We hadn't had the chance for introductions, and it was unlikely we would, so I just rolled with it.

"There must be a way. If they were trapped under the ley lines, someone trapped them there. And if they did it once, we can do it again. We need to go to her," Caleb said, turning to me.

I nodded. If she couldn't help me with my problem, I didn't know how she could help with this bigger problem. On the other hand, Mother Red Cap was hundreds of years old and had a library twice as old. She might not know, but she could at least put us on the right track. Or so I hoped.

"Who? I'm coming with you," Winston said.

"I think we all are. We can't separate now," the guy said and looked behind him at the remaining witches for support.

"No," I said, and he looked at me. "You can't come with us."

"Why not?"

Were we going to have a problem? I wasn't in the mood for a cock fight, but if he wanted to feel like the leader and question me, I'd have to put him in his place.

Caleb stepped in between us and raised his hands.

"Ashton, you can't come. We have to do this alone. I can't exactly explain why, but we need to speak to someone and the only way she will is if we go alone."

Ashton? Where had I heard that name before? There weren't many people called Ashton, surely. The only one I knew of sprung to mind.

Ashton Beauchamp? The famous author? No, it couldn't be. If the award-winning thriller writer was a witch, the force would have caught a whiff of it, right? Unless we were absolutely useless at finding any witches without the high council's aid.

"And what do you expect us to do, Caleb? Sit tight and wait while humans are dying?" Ashton said.

"I can't believe I'm saying this, but I agree with him," Winston added.

"There's something you can do. Something all of you can do," I said, stepping into the center of the room.

"What?" Ashton asked.

Instead of answering his question, I looked at Winston.

"Call Lloyd. Tell him it's time to come out of hiding."

"But, Wade," Caleb said. "It's dangerous. He and the others will be helpless against the demons."

"They don't have to fight the demons. They only have to face what they're good at."

"What exactly are we talking about?" Ashton asked.

Graham spoke for the first time since the demons had left with the high council.

"He wants the witch hunters to get back in business." The hatred was apparent in his tone.

I shook my head.

"No. I want them to help us take down a national threat before it becomes international."

"Forget about it." Graham groaned. "We're not working with hunters."

"Why not?" Ashton asked.

He was starting to grow on me. Maybe he wasn't that bad after all.

"What do you mean why not? They're witch hunters," Graham replied.

"If witches can side with genocidal demons, witches can work with hunters."

"Ash, stay out of this," Graham said.

"And what? Leave you to deal with it? I think you've had your chance, and you screwed it up." He turned to me. "If we go to them, why would they help us."

"Because I ask them to," Winston said. "Because Christian destroyed everything, and they need something to believe in."

"Guys," Caleb shouted and all eyes turned to him. "You're forgetting something important. We're not facing a couple of kids throwing tantrums. We're up against highly skilled, highly trained witches. No matter how much training hunters have, they don't know how to go up against anything like the high council."

"Then let's give them an advantage," I said.

Caleb cocked his head in confusion.

"We used to use swords laced with blood magic, right? Even though we thought they were laced with angel blood. How about we lace their swords with magic?"

"Are you out of your mind? How would you do that? And why? So that once this is all over, they can kill us all?" Graham said.

"Considering we don't know if we'll survive any of this, that's a pretty big theoretical question," Ash said.

"As for the how," I added. "I'm sure you can whip something up."

Graham turned on the spot, looking for the person I was talking to, despite knowing full well I was talking to him.

"No," he said.

"Yes," said everyone else.

"Listen, we don't have much time to lose, so you guys go find the hunters. Wade and I will find answers," Caleb said and walked out of the room.

"I'll call you to give you an update," Winston said as I followed Caleb.

The bloodbath in the corridors shouldn't have done anything to creep me out. After all, I'd killed enough times to not give blood a second thought.

Yet, somehow, thankfully, I still felt a sadness about

the innocent deaths of these people. Had they not been good enough to help Christian, or whoever was in Christian's body? Did they not deserve to choose a side before they died? Or was Christian purposefully after the strong, powerful witches?

We took the lift, and once the door closed, Caleb leaned on the wall of the elevator.

"Are you okay?" I asked him.

I knew the answer even without touching him.

"It's not your fault, Caleb. None of this is your fault. Or mine. It's all Christian and Danielle's doing. She's the one you should be pissed at."

Caleb smiled, even through his sad eyes, and leaned his head on my shoulder.

"How do you even know what I'm thinking?"

"Because I can read you like an open book," I said, but he didn't respond.

Silence permeated the lift for a few moments while we recomposed ourselves.

"What if we can't put an end to this?" he eventually asked.

I turned to face him, and he lifted his head so he could look into my eyes.

"We will," I whispered, placing my hand to his cheek and caressing it with my thumb. "And even if we don't, we'll die trying."

It wasn't the most romantic thing to say to your boyfriend, but as far as pep talks went, it wasn't the worst.

Ah, who was I kidding. I'd tanked it. That didn't mean Caleb didn't let himself feel liberated by my words.

I leaned in to give him a kiss and the doors opened.

"Let's go find Mother Red Cap," he said.

And so we did. We took a cab right outside The Shard, and it carried us all the way to Camden. The roads were busy, and every other mile we had to let another ambulance or police car overtake.

London wasn't sleeping tonight. The radio station in the taxi kept sharing the tally of deaths from the club and the Thames tsunami, as the media had dubbed what had happened on the riverside.

The driver attempted to start up a conversation about the terror attacks, but neither of us had any energy to carry a conversation and pretend we didn't know what was going on.

When we reached the canal, it felt like a lifetime had passed and like we were still faced with the same troubles.

Caleb sacrificed a spell on the bottom of the river, and unlike my last visit to her, she didn't take long to answer.

"I presume you've seen the news?" Caleb said as soon as he walked through the door.

She was hunched over her desk, deep in concentration. Caleb went and stood beside her, and only then did she lift her gaze and acknowledge us.

"It's a terrifying night tonight," she said.

"You ain't heard nothing yet." He told her what had happened at the high council hearing.

She was struggling to stand by the time Caleb finished the story.

"You-you're sure they said Ealistair and Rhafnet."

Caleb helped her take a seat on her desk chair and reached out for a glass of water on the table to pass to her.

"Yes," he said.

"Who the fuck are Ealistair and Rhafnet?" I asked.

They'd told us they were the creators, but surely if they were, I'd have heard of them.

"Demons," Caleb said at the same time as Mother Red said, "Gods."

"Demons, gods, same difference really," Mother Red Cap said. "They were deities, some say the first witches. Ealistair, the master of fire, and Rhafnet, the mistress of death, the raven goddess. When they came together, their power surged, and their union made them unstoppable. They gifted magic to the world, and that's how witches were born."

"But that's just a myth," Caleb muttered. "Right?"

I sat down by the fire pit and looked into the flames.

"They didn't look like a myth to me," I said.

"You're right. If they're here, they're real," she said.

"How do we stop them?" Caleb asked, taking a few steps back so he was at equal lengths between Mother Red Cap and me.

"You can't. They're gods," I said.

"Even gods can die," Caleb said.

I admired his confidence and relentlessness. But I'd hoped Mother Red Cap would tell us they were some deranged witches or ghouls possessing Christian's and Hew's bodies, and all we needed was a good exorcism. Not confirm they were the creators of witches. How could we even go up against that?

"We are the second coming," I said, remembering what those witches in the alley had said before I'd accidentally murdered them.

"What?" Caleb asked.

"That's what they said, the witches I chased."

"What witches?" Mother Red asked, so I told her what happened back at Westminster when I went after that gang.

Caleb nodded. "I just realized. Graham's spell didn't work, did it?"

"I'm doomed," I sighed.

"You're not doomed," Mother Red Cap said.

"Sure I am. Do you know how many spells I've used over the years? Hundreds. If I can't stop them and I have to ride it out like you suggested, I'll be putting everyone in danger."

It was so frustrating that I was still dealing with the same issue when we had much bigger fish to fry.

"Like it or not, those spells saved your life," Caleb said. "We'll just have to find a way to help you control them."

"He doesn't have to," she said from her hunched position over her chair. "These...outbursts are his body's way of accepting his new self. When it has, and *he* has, the outbursts will stop."

"Accepting what new self?" I asked.

"I second that question," Caleb added.

Mother Red Cap took a big breath as if she needed it to deal with our idiocy and got off her chair.

"Don't you think it's a little strange that all this started happening since the surge? The surge that ignited all the witches across London?" she said.

"We know that. That's what we've been saying. That this ley line surge has caused my body to go haywire and those spells to activate," I said.

"Are you saying he's a..." Caleb said. "No. Graham would have sensed it."

"Sensed what?" I asked.

"I don't know how your high priest's powers work," Mother Red said, "but would you be surprised if he wasn't entirely attuned to hearing out your witch-hunter friend? Sometimes we don't want to see what's right in front of us, no matter how much it slaps us in the face."

I was starting to get frustrated with them. Why did they not say outright what they wanted to say?

"I'm a what?" I asked.

Both Caleb and Mother Red turned to me at the same time.

"A witch," they said, and the room stilled.

What were they talking about? I couldn't be a witch. Since when? My outbursts were driving them to the wrong conclusion, and I didn't know what to say or how to feel.

"I'm not a witch. The spells I used are just going awry."

"He's right," Caleb said and looked back at Mother Red Cap.

She rolled her eyes and put her hands on her hips.

"It's like I'm talking to Dumb and Dumber all of a sudden. My darlings, do you see any of my spells going…haywire?" she asked and pointed around the room. "If the ley lines were causing spells to go off, whether inhaled or stored, wouldn't we all be having problems?"

"Oh," Caleb said. "I didn't think of that."

"You're wrong. I'm not a witch. It's just my body reacting to the dust and the surge. That's what it is. Don't make this weirder than it is. You're wrong."

"Fine," Mother Red Cap said and stretched her hands to the side to show her surrender. "But don't come back to me crying if I'm not."

Me? A witch? No fucking way.

Thirteen

Caleb

W as it possible Wade was a witch? He'd never known his father, so there was a chance there was a truth in that.

But if he was a witch, so was Winston, right? And I hadn't heard Hew talk about Winston showing any signs of natural powers.

"Any luck?" I asked as Mother Red Cap browsed her bookcase, looking for any books that could tell us more about the demons that had taken up Christian's and Hew's bodies.

She flopped on her chair in a dramatic manner and shook her head.

"Everything leads to a dead end. It's been hundreds of years since their legend was alive. I'm not surprised nothing's been written about them in the last few centuries, but I really thought I had something."

"But there must be something, otherwise how

would Danielle know about them and how to awaken them," I said.

Her scheming finally made sense. All this time we were made to believe that she had sided with Christian to take revenge for her girlfriend's death, punishing the people that had assigned her the mission to kill Christian, but all this time she'd not only meant to tap into the ley lines but also release the demons that would bring about the witch apocalypse.

Did she really want the high council on her side? Probably not. There was little she could do now that the demons were out of their cage and called the shots. She might have been the mastermind behind Christian's demise, but she was definitely no longer in control.

And she was still bitter about Hew taking on Rhafnet's spirit. Maybe we could find a way to use that to our advantage.

"I have no idea," Mother Red Cap said and sighed, but then, the next moment, she flew out of her chair and opened her drawers like a maniac. She retrieved a flyer.

"Everything okay?" I asked as her eyes glazed over and the smugness returned to her face.

"I knew I'd seen it somewhere," she said and tapped the flyer with her finger. "There's a section in the British Library. An exhibition on ancient gods."

Wade stood up and came to stand by my side.

"That's it? An exhibition at the British Library?

And you guys are wondering how Danielle found out about them?" He shook his head.

"It's not a normal exhibition," she said. "It's an ancient collection they retrieved from a newly discovered archaeological site on the Isle of Wight. They've been trying to preserve it since they found it, and they're hoping to put it on show within the next few months, but they keep pushing the date because the artifacts are proving...temperamental."

"If they're not on display yet, how did Danielle find out—" I said, but then I remembered the file Graham had handed me a few days after Christian's demise on that rooftop. "She works there. She's a curator of new content or something."

"And she probably inspected the preservation process. Maybe something caught her attention and she found the information she needed," Mother Red Cap said.

"If that's the case," Wade said, "and you were Ealistair and Rhafnet, would you let those artifacts survive?"

"They might not know how she found out," I said.

Mother Red Cap clapped her hands together once in such an unprecedented manner that I thought for a moment she, too, had been possessed.

"She probably hasn't told them so she can keep an ace up her sleeve. In case things go...awry."

I nodded. That was entirely possible. And clever of

her. Of course, it would have been cleverer if she'd never awakened those demons in the first place.

"I guess we're going on a trip to the British Library," Wade said, and I winked at him.

"See? I told you we can kill a god."

He laughed.

"If there was ever anyone who could do it, that'd be you, babe," he replied and hope mixed with want flared in my stomach.

We could still put an end to this.

———

We left the den and came out in Camden where Wade proceeded to call Winston and update him.

"Don't mention where we're headed," I whispered to him.

"Yeah, we might have a way to stop them. I'll let you know... I don't know. I'm sure he'll be fine... Of course, we'll do everything to get him back," he said and hung up.

"Worried about Hew?" I said, and he nodded.

"Why didn't you want me to say anything about the British Library?"

I shrugged.

"We don't know what these assholes are capable of. Let the wrong thing slip to the wrong person at the wrong time and we could be ruining our chances of putting an end to this."

"Makes sense. Are you ready for this? Breaking into the British Library won't be easy."

I hailed a cab and one screeched to a stop in front of us. I opened the door and settled next to him.

"Look at you!" I said. "A month ago, you didn't want to break the law, and now, you don't give a damn."

I couldn't help but laugh. Even with an army of witches and witch hunters on our back, he'd been reluctant to break into Ash's home and steal the ingredients necessary for the transference spell.

"Well, if it's to stop a genocide, I'll do anything," he said.

I pursed my lips in an attempt at a smile. As much light as I was making of the situation, this was serious. If we failed, we wouldn't just be losing our lives. But millions of people would die or be enslaved to a ruthless couple of gods.

"I've got more than enough spells to keep luck on our side," I said and pulled my sleeves up to reveal my latest upgrade. I'd ordered the gauntlets a few days ago and worn them for the first time today.

While my old spellbooks had the capacity for ten small spells in total, my new gauntlets could hold up to sixteen on each hand. I'd spent the whole morning organizing the spells so I was prepared for the worst. I was super excited with the result. The best part was they provided extra warmth on my hands with the wool coating inside.

"Those are awesome," Wade said. "Why didn't you show me earlier?"

"Didn't get a chance, did I? Anyway, after everything that's happened in the last few weeks, I didn't want to be caught defenseless ever again. You like the gauntlets? Wait 'til you see the spells they're carrying." I pulled my sleeves back down again.

"I need to arm myself again. I've told Winston to get me a sword. I hope you don't mind."

I scooted up closer to him and put my hand around his thigh.

"Why would I mind? We need all the help we can get."

"He said Graham has managed to create magic repellent spells on the swords."

"Of course he did. He's good at what he does," I said, but I didn't feel good saying it.

If there was ever a person who was more in the gray than Graham, I would love to meet them. What made his situation more upsetting was the fact he thought he was white, pure good, when his actions had been made of something evil.

"That will be fifteen quid," the driver said, bringing us both out of our stupor.

I looked outside and saw the red-bricked buildings that made up the British Library.

I tapped my card on the card reader, and we both got out of the cab. It was late and the streets were quiet, despite the few travelers lugging their suitcases to Kings Cross and St. Pancras.

We walked across the street, towards the courtyard in the front entrance, but once we turned the corner, Wade grabbed my arm and pulled me back.

"What?" I asked.

He glanced at the front door, and I turned to peek around the wall we were hiding behind to see what he'd spotted.

And thank goodness for his preparedness and hardcore training because a few more steps and they would have seen us.

Men in black clothes holding batons that doubled as spellbooks were pacing and keeping watch of the entryway. A little further investigation revealed the rest of the guards on the rooftops and around the perimeter.

"You think Danielle told them about the exhibit?" Wade whispered.

I shrugged. I didn't know why she would be that stupid to tell them. Or maybe she wasn't and she had hired her own muscle to protect the artifacts. Who knew?

"We'll need backup," I said.

"On the way," Wade replied and shook his phone.

We gathered on the street around the corner, away from all the attention the library was getting with all the security detail.

It was the most bizarre thing to see a place full of books under so much protection. The bookworm in Annabel would have loved to see that. The worried witch in me, though, was concerned how we'd get through all these people.

And once we were inside? What did we do once we were in?

Focus, Caleb. One thing at a time.

"Right, is everyone clear what they need to do?" I asked and looked at everyone.

Winston and Ash were standing next to each other. Graham was standing next to me and didn't look any happier working with hunters. Lloyd was behind Winston in a little circle with a couple of hunters. Wade even farther away, next to the other high council members. In the front, the rest of the witch hunters, about twenty men or so and a handful of women, testing their new, enhanced swords.

Everyone nodded, and I felt like I was back in the army. Only in the army, I hadn't been a general, and that's what I felt like now with so many faces looking to me for commands.

"Wade, Ash, and the rest of the high council, you're with me. Lloyd and his team, you're our backup. Winston, you are on the outside taking those bitches down."

Okay, it was wildly different than the army. If anyone had said that back then, there'd have been a snigger or a chuckle. These people remained unaffected.

"Actually," Ash said. "Win and I were talking, and I think I'd be better suited for your backup."

Win? Since when was Winston 'Win?'

"Ash, you're not trained for battle—" I started to rationalize with him.

"Don't you worry. I know how to use my power for war." He grinned.

I didn't know how a pheromone-inducing power could be used for battle, but I'd love to see what he had in mind.

"Fine. Ash, you're our backup. The rest stays as is," I said, and Ash winked at me.

I turned around and walked down the road while everyone behind me took their positions.

We crossed the street and waited behind a tree, not caring much for cover, waiting for Winston to get into place.

Only moments later, he walked up to the guards with his hands stretched out and shouting from the top of his lungs.

"I wanna see my mamma," he slurred. "Where is my mamma? Get her now."

I stifled the laughter I had bubbling up, but not the smile when the guards tried to push him away.

From his right hand, a blade stretched out in a

flash, and before the two guards in front of him knew what was happening, they dropped to the ground.

"All I wanted was my mamma. I didn't even get to ask about my daddy," he shouted, and he now had the attention of all the guards on site.

"Your brother makes an excellent drunk," I told Wade, and he chuckled.

"Yeah, can't say he hasn't had experience with the role."

Within seconds, Winston was surrounded by guards with spells in their hands. One of them cast their spell, but Winston cut at it with his sword, making the dust and smoke disappear before it had the chance to manifest.

Before anyone else could cast a spell to hurt him, the witch hunters came out from the shadows with their swords raised and ready to attack. The guards had surrounded Winston and the hunters surrounded the guards.

What followed wasn't particularly pleasant, but it did the job and kept the security detail in the front busy.

"How is that better than what Ealistair and Rhafnet are planning to do?" Graham asked, his disapproval obvious.

"What was it you'd said? We sacrifice the few to save the many?" I said, and I could tell he didn't like my answer. "We're at war, Graham. They picked their side, we picked ours. Now we fight."

I watched as one of the hunters picked up a walkie-talkie from one of the fallen guards and spoke into it. Soon, the guards from the back of the building joined the fight.

"That's our cue," Wade said, and we ran.

We got to one of the back entrances that had been guarded not too long ago, and Graham pressed a spell on the door, muttering "unlock" under his breath, and the door clicked open.

Lloyd, Ash, and the rest of the team entered first to scope out, and once they gave us the all clear, Wade, Graham, and I followed behind.

We entered a dark corridor and climbed the steps. The door at the top of the staircase was open and our backup team had their swords out at the ready, with their backs to us, making a circle as we came out.

"What is it?" I whispered.

"We heard something," Ash answered.

Wade extended the blade of his sword and looked around him. I couldn't see anything, and I couldn't help, so I let them do their job.

"Graham, did you bring it?" I asked.

He nodded, and we stepped back out onto the staircase to look at the schematics he'd retrieved before he got here. I used my phone's screen as a torch to read the floor plans.

"The restoration department is right here, at the back, on level -3 of section C. That's where the manuscripts will be. But I hope you know there will be spells around them. The guards will not be the only protection," Graham said.

"Well, that's exactly what your job is. To deactivate them. Did you make the shielding spells I asked you to?"

He nodded with a grimace.

"We don't have much choice, Graham. You heard them. They want to destroy humanity."

"You are the one who accused me for justifying a wrong with a righteous attitude," he said. "And now you're doing the same thing."

"Look how the tables have turned, huh," I said. "If you're so against what we're doing, why didn't you join your fucking gods?"

I'd had enough of his bullshit and him looking down on everything I did and any decision I made.

"How are we doing over there?" I asked the others.

Wade joined us and kneeled down.

"We think someone's playing mind games, so Lloyd wants to be cautious."

"We don't have much time. If Danielle, or, worse, the demons get a whiff of what we're doing, we're toast," I said.

"I'm on it," Ash said, louder than expected, and he extended the blade of his sword. "Time for Ash to play."

He gave me a wink, and I braced myself. This wasn't going to be easy to explain to these people after.

I watched Ash turn from a normal witch to a

divine creature that emanated light. It was as if I was a ship and he was the lighthouse I was meant to avoid, but which I wanted to crash into so desperately. My breath slowed and the blood traveled down to my cock, giving me an instant boner, reminding me of the times we'd spent in bed and the countless orgasms he'd made possible.

I wanted to check on the others, but it was impossible to look at anyone but him. I could see Lloyd and his team were suffering a fate similar to mine.

"I need you here. Now," Ash said, and his voice was not just a song, but also a command. One I couldn't help obeying. I got to my feet and walked closer to him, brushing shoulders with Wade and Graham, and soon we were all hunched around Ash and his irresistible charm.

"Step aside. I only need him," Ash said, and again I took a step back and watched as the others followed the same order.

When the space around him cleared, I saw the man opposite him take slow steps towards Ash, unable to stop himself.

The man finally stood right in front of Ash, and Ash gave the man his sword.

No. I wanted to shout. I wanted to stop him. What was he doing?

"Now, kill yourself," he ordered the guy, and we all watched as the man placed the hilt in front of his heart and retracted the blade over it.

It was like I'd felt the pull of a magnet, and all of a sudden, that magnet stopped working. Ash looked like his normal self again, and I had control of my body.

I turned to Wade, who was staring at Ash as if he was still under his lure.

"What the fuck?" one of the hunters said.

"Remind me to never piss you off," Lloyd said and nudged Ash's shoulder.

"What is wrong with you, Ashton? When did you become heartless?" Graham shouted, and I rushed to shut his mouth with my palm.

The guy might be dead, but there were still others around.

"Since this guy was a convicted murderer who had miraculously escaped prison. The work of my lovely colleagues at the council I'm sure."

"Who is this guy?" Wade whispered in my ear.

"In the human world? He's an author. In the witch world? He's an attorney for magical affairs. He's the man whose house we robbed."

"What? The man you were hired to protect?"

I nodded.

"He doesn't look like he needs protection."

"Trust me, he does," I said, and we started moving again before I could explain to him. It wasn't the right time to explain anyway.

We moved north, towards section C, and with the help from Lloyd, Ash, and their backup team, we took down more of the security witches inside.

Once we got to section C, we took the stairs down, and when we finally came to the restoration department, we put Graham to work.

"Work your craft, old man," I said.

"You know, these old-man comments are getting exhausting. I'm not even a hundred yet."

"Fine. Get to work, young man," I corrected and let him take down the protection spells in the room.

"It's done," he said only moments later.

"Already?" I asked.

Graham smiled mischievously, like I'd never seen him do before, and rolled up his sleeves.

"I'm not a high priest for nothing, boy."

"No comment," was all I managed as I opened the door to let everyone in. Wade stepped in first, and before anyone else could walk in, a blue energy ball flashed and hit Wade right in the chest.

"No!" I shouted and jumped closer to him, already retrieving a spell from my gauntlet, which I immediately threw to the right in the direction of the witch who had attacked him.

The chaos spell swallowed him up and gave me a chance to get to Wade, who, despite the attack, was still standing.

"Are you okay?" I asked.

He turned to look at me, and I expected to see him wincing, grimacing, or something to denote pain. I expected to see blood somewhere or burns from the electric charge of the energy ball. Something, anything. But there was nothing.

"I'm...I'm fine."

"How is that possible?" Graham shouted and stepped inside too.

Maybe there was merit in Mother Red Cap's words. Was Wade a witch? Or was this another outburst that had ended up protecting him from harm?

"I...we...we think he's a witch," I said, and both Wade and Graham looked at me like I was crazy.

"I'm not a witch."

"He's not a witch," both Wade and Graham said at the same time.

"It was just another outburst," Wade said.

"I would know if he was a witch," Graham said.

"How else do you explain what's happening?" I asked.

Lloyd stepped inside the department, followed by Ash and the rest of the hunters.

"Sorry, guys, are we interrupting some family drama? Are we here to steal something or recreate your favorite soap opera?" Lloyd said.

"He's right." Wade was quick to agree and looked around him. "Everybody look around for some really old shit."

"You're not helping," Lloyd said. "Everything looks old."

I turned in the direction of the witch still battling

with the chaos spell. He'd be busy for a while. I walked around him and inspected the artifacts closest to him.

As expected, there was a glass case with a very old-looking book inside, written in a language I could not even begin to pretend to understand.

I walked around the case and looked for any clues. I'd known this plan wasn't going to be foolproof, but I hadn't thought we'd get stuck on the most important part.

Graham also made circles around with me, admiring the pages of the book, and Wade just watched us, trying to figure it out.

"Is this it?" Graham asked.

I wanted to reply with a "How the fuck am I supposed to know?" when I spotted it. A little label on the corner of the glass.

Artifact 332—1928/Isle of Wight, Demonology of Old Britain.

"This is it," I said remembering the title of the upcoming exhibition.

"Great," Graham said and placed two crystals at the left corners of the display and then walked around to place two more opposite.

"Absorb and protect," he said, and the glass rippled.

I hadn't known how he was going to do this, but now that I watched his spell take full effect, I had a newfound respect for his power.

The glass disappeared in a whirl, swallowed by the

book, and the dust residue from the stones encased the entire tome and made it glow.

Within seconds a book that had to be kept in perfect conditions to stop it from decaying was exposed in the middle of an empty surface at normal room temperature, thanks to Graham's spell.

"Okay, see, now that was cool." Lloyd whistled just as my chaos spell expired and the witch came out of its daze, but ready for a fight.

Lloyd didn't even bother to look at him as he stabbed him with his sword, and the witch dropped dead next to him.

"We got it. Now what?" he asked as if nothing had happened.

Fourteen

Getting the book had been a task and a half. When Winston and his team had surrounded the guards, they'd had the upper hand, but as much protection as the swords Graham had laced could offer, they couldn't do much against the witches' natural powers. Winston lost three hunters, and as much as I wanted to stay behind and console him, we all had jobs to do. His job was to clean up the mess at the British Library before it opened again in the morning, and Caleb's and my job was to get the book back to Mother Red Cap and get it translated.

Which was easier said than done. Not only did she have to find the right dictionary, but she also had to put together a spell to translate the book for us, but to do that, she'd have to bypass Graham's protective spell.

Caleb and I rested by the fire pit while she was hard at work in her lab with the book.

"So," I said to Caleb once Mother Red Cap had informed us she wouldn't be much longer. "Tonight, I've met your ex and the boyfriend of another. You've had a few, haven't you?"

It hadn't been an easy night, and the thought had been bugging me since I'd seen Ash's irresistible power, but it hadn't been the right time to say anything. Not that now it was, but it was better than sitting in silence licking our wounds.

"Does that bother you?" Caleb said.

Did it bother me? I didn't know. I didn't care that he had a past. And I wasn't going to be jealous of the men he'd been with. They were all there. In the past.

"I don't think so," I said.

"But?"

"But..." I started, and I looked at him, his gray eyes had taken on an orange hue from the reflection of the flames. "It makes me think. When will you get bored of me?"

It sounded and felt wrong saying it, but if I was going to be honest with him, I had to tell him how I felt.

Caleb bit his lip and frowned.

"You...you think I dumped them? You think I got bored and moved on to the next toy?"

I tried to cut in and tell him no, but he didn't let me.

"I never want to fall in love, Wade, but fucking hell, I do. A lot. And every time my heart gets twisted and pulled in all directions and then put through the fucking shredder for good measure."

"What...what do you mean?"

"You know about Jin, but I've never told you about anyone else. Jin wasn't my first, but he was my first love. And he was taken away from me in the most brutal way. And then it was Anthony, the cyclops."

"Maximilian's boyfriend."

My comment took him by surprise. "Boyfriends? When I met them both they were just good buddies. I must have missed a few episodes. Anyway, yes, Anthony was the first guy I met after Jin. Of course, I didn't know at the time that I'd met and lost you in the interim. I just knew there was a year's worth of memories missing, and I didn't know how to get them back.

"Anthony was good, but I was still grieving Jin's loss two years later. For me, it'd only been a year. You know? He stayed with me for six months, and I let myself love him. I had my empathy by that time, so I could tell he loved me, and he wanted something more. But I couldn't abandon Nora and Annabel. I had a responsibility towards the woman who'd saved my life, and I couldn't leave my best friend to take care of her.

"But Anthony wanted to move in together, wanted a family of his own. Wanted things from me that I wasn't ready to give him. I already had a family. I never really told anyone what Nora really was, so he couldn't understand why I couldn't let her go. I can't blame him. When he got with me, he'd thought he was only getting me, not a whole package deal."

"He didn't like Nora?"

I didn't know how anyone could say no to Nora and her charming little self, or how anyone couldn't like Annabel and her no-bullshit attitude.

"No. It wasn't just Nora. It was my life. Graham was hiring me for jobs all the time for the high council. Spying and things like that. He didn't like what I was doing. Found it dishonest. So one day, he knocked on my door and told me he was done. He accused me of still being hung up on Jin, and that it had made me into something he didn't like."

"Fuck that shit. And you wanted to get rid of your emotions because of him? He sounds like an asshole. Which is a shame because Maximilian looks like a nice guy."

Caleb shook his head.

"It's not his fault. I am a lot to take on. And it's not just Anthony. It's a series of guys who all couldn't be with me for one reason or the other. Ash was the last guy I put my faith in, until...until you."

I took his gloved hand and squeezed it between mine.

"What did Ash do?" I asked, not sure if I wanted to hate the guy.

"Graham hired me to protect this high-powered, high-class witch who had a stalker."

"A stalker? Surely he could do what he did back there and make him disappear."

Caleb looked into the flames and took a deep breath.

"He is powerful. If he wasn't, he wouldn't be a member of the high council, but his power comes at a cost. He can only manipulate people's pheromones for so long before they lose their mind. And even if he doesn't use it for long, as soon as they're out of his radius, whatever he's asked them to do doesn't matter anymore.

"Which is how he got his stalker. Someone got addicted to the pheromone overload and lost their mind, so they started doing things no normal human being would do," Caleb said.

"Okay." I urged him to go on.

"So, I did. I protected him. But if you put an empath and a siren in the same room, things are bound to go kaboom."

"And they did?"

"They did. We slept together. He used his power on me; I used my power on him. We had a wild run. And I'd thought it could last longer than the job. You know? Maybe we could keep seeing each other. But Ash...Ash would never be caught dead with someone like me."

"How do you know?".

"Because he told me. He said what we had could never be anything more because he could never present me to anyone. He had a status and a reputation to uphold."

"I knew he was a douchebag!"

"Yeah." He shrugged. "So I walked out on him and on the job."

"Good. He doesn't deserve your protection with that attitude."

"Too bad the council didn't see it that way."

"Fuck the council."

"Fuck the council," he agreed, and then silence filled the room once again. The only sound the crackling of the wood in the fire.

"The reason why I'm telling you all this is not because I want you to hate all my exes. It's because I want you to understand that no one's ever lasted, and I didn't have much say in it. It's not because I'm a player. It's because I haven't found someone who will take me as I am, bruises and all. The only ones who did ended up dead. Do you understand what I'm saying? I'm not going to get bored of you, Wade. But you might get bored of me, or I might lose you, and if I do, I don't know what I'll do."

How could I have been so stupid? How could I have thought that Caleb's feelings weren't genuine. I'd been inside his head, had felt his emotions like he'd felt mine. I was an A-grade idiot for even starting on the subject, but at least now I knew. I knew that he was the guy I was meant to be with.

"I'm not going to get bored of you, okay?" I said.

"And even if I die, I'll find my way back to you. I'll haunt you if I have to." I put my hand on his cheek and turned his head so I could kiss those beautiful lips I'd missed kissing and stare into those handsome eyes I'd missed staring into.

"Glad to see you've kept busy." I heard Mother Red Cap behind us, and we both turned to look at her.

She was carrying the demonology book, which she placed on her desk. We rushed to our feet and huddled around the book, which now looked to be written in plain English.

"You've already cast the spell?" Caleb asked.

"It took precision and attention, but yes. It makes for an interesting read."

Caleb leaned over the book and started reading:

"Before the age of man, a man made of fire and steel walked the earth. He wandered for hundreds and hundreds of years until mankind was born, looking for his one true love, but all he ever came upon was death and destruction.

"They named him the god of war because all he ever left behind him was blood and tears. His true name was Ealistair.

"One day, after a battle that nearly cost him his life, a raven came to him as he bled to death, and it fed on his blood. His power gave the raven so much strength that it turned into a beautiful woman unlike anything he'd ever seen. And she nursed him back to health by feeding him her blood. They were linked for life.

"Together they brought about the demise of kings and tormentors. They set slaves free, but there was something missing from their life.

"A child. After centuries of being together, they brought a daughter to life the same way the raven goddess, Rhafnet, had brought her husband back from certain death. And so Avalis was born.

"Avalis might have been made of blood and death, but she ruled with love and generosity. Her parents tried to raise her with their values, but her compassion broke through the darkest of days. She could bring to life anything that died.

"Rhafnet and Ealistair saw the beauty they'd created and had a vision of a world full of children like Avalis. The two parents came together and whispered the secrets of the universe to humans. No one had done that ever before. Those humans became something different, something else. They mastered powers beyond the physical realm. They became a mirror image of the gods that had created them.

"Avalis watched as the world became wrought with witches who took advantage of their powers to bring more destruction and chaos to the world. The witches, her parents' creations, were nothing like her. They went against everything Avalis was and believed in. They didn't help the world become a better place. They made it worse.

"When the witches took her lover away from her, the man she had chosen to marry and share a life with, a man her parents did not approve of, Avalis became enraged. She couldn't see any more witches take what wasn't rightfully theirs because they had more power.

"So she cast a spell on all of them. The witches her parents had created lost their powers and they could only ever get them back by a process of ignition. If they wanted to be more than human again, they'd have to pass her tests. Then, and only then, would she grant them their powers back.

"Rhafnet and Ealistair were not happy. They'd hoped their daughter would rule by their side, but she betrayed their trust. They schemed to kill her and stop her from ruining their plans. The child they'd once longed for was now their mortal enemy.

"But Avalis's compassion and love made her stronger than death. When Rhafnet and Ealistair came to murder her, she sacrificed herself to keep her parents from ever hurting anyone else. And so both husband and wife became trapped in the confines of the earth, where the secrets of the universe converged.

"And as for Avalis, she gave up her mortal body so her spirit could transcend and keep guard over her parents so they could never be free," Caleb said, his voice croaky by the time he'd finished.

"Avalis," I said. "She's our only hope, right?"

Mother Red Cap nodded, and Caleb turned the pages of the book.

"But how? If she was meant to protect the ley lines and her parents are free, something's happened to her, right?" he asked.

"This is just a story, my dear boy. Everything is open to interpretation."

"I've never heard of Avalis," Caleb said. "I've heard Rhafnet mentioned before and Ealistair, but never her name."

"It wouldn't be the first time the witches erased history to rewrite on their own terms. My guess is someone didn't like the original and wrote Rhafnet and Ealistair with Avalis's qualities, as the loving, compassionate gods that created witches," Mother Red said.

"But now what? How do we invoke her?" I asked.

Caleb leafed through the pages faster than necessary.

"I think...I think I found it," he said and read the passage. "Just like Avalis was made of blood and love, so can she be invoked in the same way. But be warned. Only a witch of immense power can take on her spirit."

"Blood and love. What does that mean?" I asked.

Caleb pursed his lips as he quietly read the rest.

"It's a sex ritual," Mother Red Cap said. "One I've not heard of before."

"Will...will you take on Avalis?" Caleb asked her, and Mother Red Cap laughed in his face.

"Me? Why would I take on her spirit?"

"To help us take Rhafnet and Ealistair down. You read what it says. Only a witch of immense power can take her on," Caleb said.

Mother Red Cap put her hand on Caleb's face and tugged at his cheek.

"The reason I survived for so long, dear boy, is because I've stayed away from witch politics."

"But this is not witch politics. We need you. They're planning on decimating humanity." Caleb pleaded with her. "You can't just sit and do nothing."

"I have and I will. But you don't need me to take them down. You've got you."

Caleb laughed and pulled away from her.

"I can't believe you're saying this. If they destroy everyone where does that leave you? You'd be no better than Graham."

"My decision is final." Mother Red Cap raised her voice. "And I won't have you challenging it."

"Where am I going to find a powerful witch to take on Avalis's spirit? Ash?"

"You don't need one. You've got yourself."

"I'm not powerful. I'm barely even a witch," Caleb said, and I hated seeing him cutting himself this short.

Mother Red Cap stepped away and got closer to her fire pit where she sat down and took a cigar out of her robes.

"Now," she said, lighting it in the fire. "If that were true, why the hell did the ley lines open?"

She had a point. Only the sacrifice of five powerful

witches could have let Christian tap into the ley lines, and Caleb had died on that rooftop, the ley lines had opened, and Ealistair and Rhafnet had been released.

"I'm not a witch of immense power. Don't make me laugh," Caleb said.

"Maybe not," I said. "But you're a witch who will do anything to stop a war."

FIFTEEN

CALEB

As much as they were trying to convince me they were right, I knew they were wrong. My death on the ley line was just a fluke that had worked because of circumstance. I was not a powerful witch, nor could I stop those demons, gods, whatever the fuck they were supposed to be.

"I can't do this," I told them and left to take some air.

It had been another long night, and I'd found myself yet again having next to no rest.

As I came out of Mother Red's den, the morning coolness hit me, right in the core, and it took me a few moments to realize why.

There was something in the air. Something completely unnatural. I didn't know if I was the only one who could feel it, but I knew I wasn't making it up.

Was this what was happening to the world? Was this the effect Ealistair and Rhafnet were having by being on this plane? How much worse could things get if they weren't stopped?

A lot.

If their history was anything to go by, fiction or not, there had to be an element of truth in there. And these beings would stop at nothing to get what they wanted. More death, more destruction, more innocent blood spilled.

"Hey," Wade called behind me a few moments later, moments that felt like decades inside my head.

I glanced at him before focusing again on the green water of the canal.

"What are you thinking?" he asked.

"How desperately I need my bed and a boatload of sleeping pills until all this goes away," I said, but Wade only shook his head disapprovingly.

"No, you're not. You wouldn't be able to live with yourself if you let the world go to shit."

"Yeah, well, there's not much I can do either way," I said and decided to walk the soreness in my legs off.

If I wasn't going to get any decent sleep, I might as well get some exercise. Not that I needed any more tension on my poor body. The non-stop adrenaline rush over the last few days had been more than enough to knock me out cold for a week straight.

"There is. You heard Mother Red Cap," he said, joining me by my side.

I blew raspberries and a jogger looked at me in a funny way.

"Is it so hard to believe you're a strong witch?" he asked.

"I don't have to believe it because I'm not. I was never the strongest at the army, or even a half-decent vampire for that matter. Why would I be a powerful witch?"

"First of all," Wade said, and he stopped me by putting the back of his hand on my chest, "that's bullshit because you killed a gang of elves all by yourself, so I bet you were a kickass soldier and vampire. And second of all"—he put his index finger under my chin and made me look at him, at his ocean blue eyes that I could get lost in for hours—"we both know you're going to do this sooner or later, so why delay the inevitable? You can't resist a good adventure, and you know it."

How had he come to know me so well over a month? Was I such an open book that he could read me without even trying? Or had he got his memories of me back and had failed to tell me?

He was right of course. I might not be a lot of things, but give me a new, shiny yarn and I'd follow it to the very end, like Theseus through the maze of the Minotaur.

"Fine," I said and turned to go back inside Mother Red Cap's den. "Let's go read that ritual."

Wade patted his chest over his heart and grinned.

"Already made a copy. Come on. Let's go," he said and gave me his hand to take.

Out of all the things you'd think a couple would be excited about trying, the last thing I'd thought would get my heart fluttering would be to hold Wade's hand in public. But it did. It was the most normal thing we'd done since we'd met.

"Do we really have to drink each other's blood?" Wade asked, grimacing.

"I don't know. Maybe. What does the ritual say?"

It's not like I had ancient sex rituals every day.

"You seem awfully unnerved by this," he said.

"I used to be a vampire, you know. So, it'll be like walking a day in the life for you, and a trip down memory lane for me."

We came out on the high street and were just about to go into the underground when an ambulance zoomed past the traffic after another one. I paused for a second and looked down the road. More ambulances and police cars had turned their sirens on and were filing down the traffic.

"Something's happened," I said. "They must have done something again."

Wade pulled his phone out and scrolled through his news app.

"Southwark Bridge has been hit. They're saying there was an earthquake that split it in two," Wade said.

"But London doesn't get earthquakes. We need to hurry. The longer we wait, the stronger they'll get."

We went underground and took the quickest route to Kensington, to Wade's house, and once we were in the security of his not-so-humble abode, he retrieved the copy he'd made of the ritual.

It didn't make for light reading, that was for sure. The majority of the ritual was normal stuff, building up to euphoria, things we did anyway. It was the next step that tripped me up, and it wasn't because of the blood involved.

"Are you ready for this?" Wade asked while I re-read the same line, and I thought I could detect some hesitance in his voice.

"Are you?" I gave his hand a squeeze. "You don't have to do this, you know. It's too soon for such a—"

"I'm fine. We don't have an option."

There was always an option. It might not be the popular one, but there was always one. And I didn't want to scare the man away or scar him for life.

"Are you sure, sure?" I repeated.

"I never thought I'd invoke a demon with an orgasm."

I laughed. Even in the darkest of times, he still had a sense of humor.

"We can make a habit of it if you enjoy it." I chuckled and gave him my hand to take. "But seriously, that's way too big a commitment. You've only just met me. Performing the mating—"

"It's fine. I want to," he said. "If I wasn't sure before, after tonight I'm certain."

This wasn't a walk-in-the-park kind of ritual, and I didn't even know if it was possible to undo it if he ever changed his mind. What I did know was that we needed to take Rhafnet and Ealistair down. We could worry about the rest later.

I guided him to his bedroom with the copy at hand. I lay down in bed, and he squeezed next to me. If it had been any other time, we'd have ripped each other's clothes off and he'd already be inside me. But this was different.

I took my gloves off and caressed his hair. If this had been a normal encounter, I'd have let him into my head the moment I touched him. But I wasn't ready for it yet. I wanted to know he was.

"If we do this, there's no turning back," I said. *If we do this, you are stuck with me. For life.*

Good, he replied. *I wouldn't have it any other way.*

I'd have loved to tell him he didn't know what he was getting himself into, but I didn't know, either. This was a whole new territory for me as it was for him.

Are you scared? he asked me.

Shitless, but I wasn't going to tell him that. *What if you change your mind? What if you get bored of me? What if—*

"Listen to me, Caleb Carlyle. I will never change my mind. I will never get bored of you. You and I?

We're meant to be, okay? We fell in love twice in a life-time. I want to make sure this time it sticks." I heard him loud and clear.

Besides, if you mate with me there's less chance of being claimed by a broody familiar, he added, and I chuckled.

Or we both get claimed by one and we make a sexy throuple. Two could play that game.

Wade's hand came up to my neck, and he wrapped it around me, giving my neck a light squeeze, and then he gave me a tender kiss.

"Never. I'm not sharing you with anyone ever again. You hear me?" He growled and my lips trembled, awakening my cock.

"Yes, master."

Mmm, I like that. Say that again.

"Claim me, master," I managed to say, but the rest came out in a flurry of laughter and hysterics. "Make me yours, master."

Wade removed his hand from my neck and slapped me.

"Don't ruin it, asshole. I was trying to set the scene here."

I don't know what you're talking about. What did I ruin? I'm still hard.

I can see that, he replied and groped me with his free hand while the one that had slapped me returned to its rightful position by my neck.

I wanted to grope back, feel his hardness, but he

didn't let me. I shouldn't have said the word "master" because he took it too literally, and now I was in trouble.

Put your hands behind your back, he said.

Are you crazy? I'm not lying on my hands. They'll go to sleep.

Both hands tightened around my sensitive spots, and my cock throbbed in his hand.

Traitor penis. Couldn't even pretend I wasn't enjoying this or something. It just had to say its piece and give Wade what he needed.

You either do it yourself, or I do it for you. Your choice, he said.

What kind of a dick Sophie's choice move was that?

Ah, who was I kidding? I wanted him to dominate me as much as I wanted him inside me.

No! I said defiantly, and his eyes glistened with need.

Oh, yeah, baby. I wasn't going down without a fight. He removed his hand from my neck and tried to push my shoulder down so I was lying on my chest, but I wasn't going to be manhandled.

I pushed him away from me, but it was like trying to keep two magnets from coming together.

He pushed his elbows against mine, bending my arms and closing the distance between us, and to make sure I didn't go anywhere, he sat on my crotch, not the worst place to take a seat, admittedly.

Wade grabbed my wrists and tried to pin them over my head. I used all my strength to push back, twisted my arm so he would release me, and I only managed the one hand, which I immediately wrapped around his neck and squeezed.

"Oh, fuck. Why are you doing this to me?" He choked.

"Because you asked for it."

Okay, fine. But you gotta go a little rougher on me. That's like being choked by a baby angel's kiss.

Is that right? I said and squeezed harder. I felt his cock grinding on my crotch, and before I could reach for it, Wade placed my hand there himself, sliding it under his jeans.

Harder, he said. *I can take it.*

Sure?

He nodded before closing his eyes and letting a groan out.

I clenched harder at his neck, and his face went red. My other hand, the one wrapped around his cock, palmed it hard, the friction of the fabric and my hand making him tense.

I could feel his orgasm rising like a glass of water that was about to overflow, and his pain, the tightness around his larynx, suffocated me too.

He came hard and fast in his pants, wetting my wrist and his underwear, and I eased the pressure on his neck as he came down for a kiss and a cuddle.

"I hate you," he said.

"No, you don't."

He raised his head to meet my gaze and grinned.

"No, I don't. You're right. Now, stop messing with me and let's make it right."

He got off me and slipped his underwear off. I wiped my hand on the duvet and watched him unzip my pants and pull them down.

Then, he proceeded to take mine and his T-shirts off and strip us both down until we were both stark naked.

Before he joined me back in bed, though, he left the room, and I lay my head back on the mattress.

It felt like a warm embrace around my body, and I appreciated it. It had been a wise choice to get him the new mattress. I couldn't wait to have wild nights of sleeping on it.

Who could have told me a week ago I'd be in bed about to have sex with my boyfriend to invoke a demon inside me? This was some weird territory we were getting into.

Wade returned to the room with a Swiss Army knife and placed it by the bed.

"Are you sure you don't want to kill me?" I asked him and laughed before he could take it personally.

I couldn't even begin to imagine how twisted this must have felt for Wade. He'd never had to do any odd crap like this with any of his lovers. Not only was he going to give himself entirely to me, but he was also going to drink human blood for the first time in his life. The least I could do was make this comfortable for him.

"I thought since we're missing the fangs, we might need this," he said and lay down on top of me, kissing my nose. "Stop worrying. It'll be fine. I'm fine."

Wasn't it damn, cotton-candy sweet of us to worry about each other like that when the world was ending out there? My heart warmed at the thought that even if it all came to an end, I'd at least have Wade by my side as my one and true mate.

He started us off with french kisses and light grinding, but the moment I made our connection two-way, his boner returned in an instant, feeding off my horniness. He sucked me off, and I sucked him off, but it was all more mechanical than anything else.

As much as we tried to deny it, we were both scared of what would happen next, but we knew what we had to do to stop the apocalypse.

"You know what?" Wade said. "No. If we're going to perform a ritual that will bind us for life, I sure as hell am not going to perform it like a robot, out of duty."

"What do you mean?"

"We're not going to have sex thinking about the million lives we'll be saving. If we're becoming true mates, let's have the best sex of our lives."

Before I could agree to it, he came back up and kissed my mouth, his tongue teasing my lips, and when that became too much torture, he used his teeth to bite and pull until I had no choice but to forget the war brewing out there and to focus on the union between us.

I grabbed his butt cheeks, and he took both our cocks in his hand, palming them with slow tender movements, his thumb massaging our glans.

I pinched his nipples and twisted until he growled like a beast in my mouth, his sound reverberating down to my core.

That's more like it, he said.

Shut up and take me.

Oh, don't you worry. I'll make you mine when it's time. He bit down on my bottom lip until I let out a sob.

Take me now, I said, and he responded with a slap on my face.

I call the shots on this one. And if you have anything to say to me, you call me master. Understood? The air rushed out of me, and my dick in his hand pulsed.

Yes, I replied, and he slapped me again.

Yes, what?

Yes, master.

He growled and squeezed my face so that my lips puckered.

Wade sat up and moved to sit on my chest and forced me to take his length in my mouth. I let the tip in, and then he released the grip on my face.

"That's it. Swallow it." He grunted and pushed his cock farther in.

His tip massaged my throat, and my gag reflex made me choke, but he didn't relent. Instead, he fucked my mouth, pinning me down to the bed.

His elation waved through me like ripples on a lake, and I instinctively reached for my own cock to rub it.

"Did I say you could touch yourself?" he shouted and pulled his cock out of my mouth to spit at me. Then he pushed it back in, harder, while I struggled to breathe and needed my own release.

I felt his orgasm again; it was rising and rising inside him, but before he could spill his seed again, he pulled out of my mouth and worked his way down my body.

He bit down on my nipples, licked my happy trail, and then took my cock in his mouth with a hunger I'd never seen in him before.

Yes, baby. Yes, master. Suck me, master. Please, I begged him and tried to grab his hair.

He didn't let me. Instead, he kept both my hands at my sides while he bobbed his head up and down my length, making me lose my breath and my patience.

He didn't give me a chance to climax because he let my dick go and pulled my hips up to lick my hole.

Don't clench, he said and spat on me before returning his tongue to rim me.

I'd never been big on the whole ass-eating thing, but if there was ever a time to convert, it was here and now under Wade's mercy.

I could get used to this treatment. Or maltreatment, to be more accurate. I'd always been too scared to take things to the next level because I didn't want to scare him away, but after today, he couldn't be scared away even if he wanted to. He was showing me more of his kinky side, and I liked it. I wondered what else we could try next. Could I convince him to learn the art of shibari with me so he could tie me up and use me as he saw fit?

He spanked me, and I looked at him.

"Focus," he yelled.

"Yes, master," I said, and before I knew what was happening, his cock was inside me, and I lost any control I had over my body.

He started slow, but soon he sped up, and all I could think about was how badly I needed my release.

It's time, he said as he pounded me.

I reached for the knife next to me and held it in my hand over my arm. Everyone always thought the neck was more pleasurable to drink from, but my experience had been otherwise. Neck cramps and severe bleeding made it more dangerous than it had to be. The arm, on the other hand, was easier to suck from, and it didn't give you a neck ache after. Or at least that's what Jin had told me. I was about to find out if he was right.

As Wade hammered his dick against my prostate and his climax was close, he looked at the piece of paper next to me and then into my eyes.

"I give myself to you, to have and to hold, to

protect and to defend. I bind myself to you for all eternity. Let my life force be your life force. Your blood, my blood," he said, and at that, I dug the blade of the knife across my arm until the blood oozed out of the cut, and Wade came inside me.

Then he leaned down and placed his lips over the gush. He winced for a moment before sucking the blood. The pain made my skin tense and my ears ring.

"I take you and you take me, to nurture and to feed, to shield and to shelter. I bind myself to you for all eternity. Let my life force be your life force. Your blood, my blood." I cried and grabbed my cock, which was tense, awaiting release, and palmed it hard until my cum shot out of me, and with it, all my strength as he continued to drink me.

With the knife still in my other hand, I cut Wade's arm, but he didn't budge or wince. I brought my lips up to him and reacquainted myself with the taste of silver and the thirst that had once been uncontrollable.

I might not have been a vampire anymore, but I felt the same thirst for him and he for me. It was like we were linked, glued together and couldn't let go of each other even if we wanted to.

I could feel his heartbeat as if it was mine, every muscle, every pain, every trickle of sweat was felt as if mine. It was like I'd grown a second heart that someone had pulled out of my body and put inside Wade's.

We'd mated. It was done. Now we were stuck together.

It was hard, but I forced myself to concentrate and remember the next part. The most important part.

I pulled my mouth away from his cut, the blood dripping down his arm, and yelled with all my might.

"Avalis, queen of passion and compassion, goddess of humanity and witchcraft, demon of despair, sister witch, I call you upon me. Your brothers and sisters need you."

As with four weeks ago when we'd woken up because of the energy blast surging from the ley lines, a bolt of lightning struck through us both, pulsing, vibrating, and making us feel more alive than we'd ever felt.

Wade coughed and removed his lips from my arm, too, but he didn't let me go. He opened his mouth and dust of all colors of the rainbow suffocated us, and the room lit up with fire and chaos, light and darkness.

I didn't know what was happening, but one moment, I was watching Wade have an overwhelming outburst of power, the residue of the spells he'd consumed, and the next, I knew exactly what was happening.

Why did you call me, brother? a voice said inside my head. A voice so serene it almost put me to sleep.

We need your help, Avalis. Your parents are about to destroy everything.

Sixteen

Wade

Being with Caleb on that level felt equal parts terrifying and exhilarating. I'd thought the whole blood drinking would have creeped me out, and it had, at first. But as soon as the first drop had hit my palate, I couldn't stop myself. I'd wanted more. Needed more. And when Caleb had drunk mine, it all finally made sense.

We weren't just doing a disgusting blood ritual for the sake of invoking Avalis. We were coming together as one. My blood becoming his blood, and his blood mine. We drank each other's life force until we didn't know where I ended and he began.

Was this what Winston had felt when he'd first set eyes on Hew? Or had Caleb and I come together on a whole new and different level than anyone ever before? I wasn't surprised when Caleb pulled away from me and the cut on my arm was no longer there. Neither was his. In their places were red scars—a circle like a burn mark that I knew we'd both carry forever.

"Did it work? Is she here?" I asked.

"Oh, she's here all right," Caleb said.

I was surprised he didn't sound different. Both Christian and Hew had sounded...possessed. Caleb sounded like Caleb.

"What is she saying?"

"She can feel Ealistair and Rhafnet. She can feel their hatred. She can take us to them," he said and gritted his teeth as if he was in pain.

I grabbed his arm, the one with the scar, and with my other hand lifted his chin.

"Hey," I said. "Are you okay?"

He winced but nodded.

"She's just...loud."

"Is there something I can do to help?"

"No. You can help me dress, though.".

"Of course. Anything." I helped him sit on the bed. "Here." I slipped his underwear back on and then put his T-shirt over his head, and he put his arms through the sleeves at the same time. His limbs were heavy like lead.

"Why am I not feeling like you?" I asked. "Other than being able to hear your heartbeat without even touching you, I feel...normal."

"You don-you don't have a whole other entity inside you. Nothing to do with...with mating," he said, finding it difficult to articulate.

"If he let me take control, he wouldn't be suffering."
A female voice spoke through Caleb's mouth. He groaned, and when he spoke again, it was in his own voice.

"What was that about?" I asked him.

"It's Avalis. She wants to get in the driver's seat. But I'm not letting her. I don't want her to take me over like Rhafnet took over Hew. She said she put him to sleep. I don't want Avalis doing the same to me."

"But isn't she supposed to be here to help? What was the point of invoking her?"

"Damn right, what was the point?" Avalis said through Caleb.

"We need to go," Caleb said. "We need to find the demons and the high council before it's too late."

"We do. I'll call the others. Where are the demons?"

"Tower Bridge. They are about to infiltrate the Tower of London and steal the Crown Jewels."

———

After calling Winston and asking him to get everyone and head to Tower Bridge, I got dressed, gave Caleb a caffeine hit, and we made our way to the city center in broad daylight.

If those demons were willing to rob the Crown Jewels in broad daylight, then their plans couldn't include caring much for the human authorities.

They'd made a threat to wipe out the humans in London, and they were going to make that a reality sooner rather than later.

"Why are they going after the Jewels? I thought they're demons. They can do anything they want," I said.

"No," Caleb said. "Avalis is saying there is a limit to their power. Ealistair feeds off war, and Rhafnet feeds of death—"

"That wasn't in the book.".

"Yeah, because that book is part reality, part fairy tale. Those two need chaos to survive, and what brings more chaos than the destruction of an entire race? But in order to do so, they need a spell that will amplify their power and reach."

"I'm scared to ask what that means."

"It means if they get their hands on the Crown Jewel they're after, the spell they need, they'll be able to kill everyone at the click of their fingers.".

"What?"

"Well, not the literal click of their fingers. We wouldn't want a copyright infringement on our asses, but you get what I mean. If they use the Jewel to amplify their powers, for every human they knock down, a hundred more will fall."

That certainly didn't sound good.

"How do we stop them?" I asked.

"We don't. Avalis will."

If he lets her. I wanted to tell him that, but I was

afraid he'd take it personally. It was best not to upset him now, right before battle. Why was he keeping the demon goddess at bay when the whole point of us performing the sex ritual and mating for life had been to bring her here so she could help us rid our world of her parents?

We took the train to Tower Bridge, but our trip was cut short when the train operator announced there had been a signal failure while we were still seven stops behind.

"She's getting impatient," Caleb growled as the train came to a stop at the next station, and we, along with lots of other passengers, decided it was better to walk the distance than to wait a century underground.

"Well, if Avalis has a better idea of how to get there, she's more than welcome to try," I told Caleb, hoping she was listening.

Caleb smirked but then touched his head as if someone had knocked him with a hammer.

"Follow me," he said and took my hand, walking us to the end of the platform. While passengers were busy following the "way out" signs, we stood in front of the marbled wall of the station like tourists trying to decipher a map.

Caleb took a peek behind him and a step forward and then put his index and middle fingers together and drew a circle on the wall, mumbling something under his breath that wasn't quite human.

The wall sizzled, and the circle he'd drawn became

a surge of fire and energy that all swirled in the middle in a chaotic mess. Caleb stepped back and gestured towards it.

"After you," he said and grinned.

It felt weird not trusting Caleb, but I couldn't. The way he acted and the way he spoke was off, even, when Avalis wasn't speaking through him. Was this what it was like being possessed? Or was I being paranoid?

"*I'm not trying to kill you. Go through,*" Avalis said and rolled Caleb's eyes, and for a moment, I could have sworn it had been a united act between the two.

I stepped through the circle and it felt as if the cells of my entire body were pulled apart and then put back together as I got out into the grounds of the Tower of London. I looked behind me and Caleb walked through the empty wall of the White Tower as if there was a door I couldn't see.

This was the second time I had teleported, and it seemed the more I did it, the less I liked it.

"Great, now what?" I asked.

"Now we find Winston and prepare for war," Caleb said and scanned the area.

A few tourists were staring at us, and who could blame them? They had just seen us appear from thin air. I'd be staring in their place.

Caleb sprinted towards the exit, and once we were out of the tower grounds and onto the riverbank, we ran towards the tunnel under the bridge. We didn't get a chance to climb the steps as we found a group huddled together.

I pulled my hilt out, ready to extend the blade at any strange or rapid movement, but Caleb continued, charging right at them. I picked up my pace to get there at the same time as him, but when Caleb got close, the group all turned, their swords shining under the limited lighting.

"Win," I said and pushed the blade back in. He did the same. "You're here already."

Behind him, I saw Lloyd's and Ash's faces. Graham was staring at Caleb and walked towards him, pushing everyone out of his way.

"What's wrong with you?" he asked Caleb.

"Nothing's wrong with me. What are you talking about?" Caleb slapped Graham's hand away when he reached out to touch him.

"Your aura is...different. Stronger."

"Ah, yeah, that. Nothing to worry about. It will help us take them down," Caleb said.

I didn't know why he wouldn't tell him the truth, but we didn't have time to talk about it because we heard an explosion from up above.

The screech of cars swerving penetrated my ears, and I had to cover them to protect them. From the corner of my eye, I caught a glimpse of a car falling from the bridge, right into the middle of the Thames.

"We need to hurry," Winston said.

I put a hand up to stop him, and with that, the rest of the guys paused behind us.

"Are you guys sure? This is going to be dangerous. We might not make it out alive," I said.

Ash stepped forward and pushed past Winston.

"It's too late for that. We're here now, so let's make it count," he said and ran up the steps.

Winston followed suit, and the rest of the remaining hunters and high council members barreled up the stairs ready to sacrifice their lives for the common good.

Caleb, Graham, and I were the only ones that didn't move. I had to make sure Caleb was going to be all right. And so did Graham.

"Caleb, you're scaring me," Graham said. "What's going on? What have you done to yourself?"

Caleb gave me a quick glance and avoided Graham's stare.

"I did what I had to do, Graham. I called on backup."

"Backup? What kind of backup?" he asked and looked behind us.

"The divine sort," Caleb answered and rushed up the steps.

Graham took a moment to look at me, cocked his head to the side with a narrowing of his eyes, and after a deep breath followed behind Caleb.

When I got to the top, I couldn't believe what I was seeing.

The entire traffic on Tower Bridge was pushed to the sides, the people inside the cars banging on the glass, begging for their lives, and pedestrians taking cover behind them.

In the middle of the bridge, Christian, Hew, Danielle, and the witches of the high council were making their way through. I looked behind me and hooded witches closed in on us. No spellbooks were on sight. This wasn't going to be a fight of wits and skill. This was going to be a battle of strength and power.

The other hunters didn't fail to notice the company behind us. All swords came swooshing out of their hilts, glowing in the daylight. The humans I could see behind the witches gasped and covered their eyes, a lot of them filming the action on their phones.

I took a step towards the witches when a woman, a BLADE recruit that had joined only months before Christian's fall, put her hand on my chest.

"This one's not your fight. We've got them," she said, and she glanced at the bigger guns behind us.

She was right. If I could help stop the demon nightmare back there, then there were more chances to save her and the others' lives.

Caleb, Ash, and Graham walked towards Ealistair and Rhafnet and the army behind them. Winston walked with and a few others a few feet short of Caleb.

I made a start to catch up with them when a flock

of giant ravens flew past me and within seconds turned into humans in a cloud of smoke and lightning.

A skulk of big red foxes raced up the steps we'd just taken, and behind them, a pack of...no, that couldn't be right.

We didn't have wolves in London. Surely not. Whether or not we did, a pack of gray wolves was here, right in front of my very eyes, and they all joined up the line for the battle for London and its humans.

One of the foxes walked beside me for a few moments before turning into Lorelai.

"Yo, what's up, mate. Ready to try not to die?" she asked as if we were going down for a shot of espresso and a spot of news.

"What is all this?" I asked, looking around me.

Lorelai put her hand through my arm and hopped next to me, her ponytail flicking left and right like it had a mind of its own.

"This, my friend—and I've decided we're friends now, by the way—is the familiars of London coming to help you take down those witches. Oh, sorry. Did I say witches? I meant bitches."

"Did you...did you rally them?"

Lorelai shrugged. "Me and a few of my connections." She pointed at a wolf and winked at him.

I thought I saw the wolf shaking his head in exasperation, but his snarl was too distracting to say for sure.

"You better go up there, tiger," she said and looked

at the front of the line where Caleb was and spanked me on the ass.

"I think I liked you better as an acquaintance," I said, raising my eyebrow, but she just laughed it off.

"Oh, shit. I forgot to call the tigers. Damn it. They're going to be pissed they missed the action. Oh well. Better luck next time."

And with a shrug, she turned back into a fox and left me to wade through a field of wolves, foxes, and ravens turned human.

The last line of raven men I passed were all darker in color with afro hair and young-looking. They must have been Hew's brothers. I didn't know why I was surprised they were there, but it did strike a chord that they'd joined us to save their brother.

"Where were you?" Caleb asked, not taking his eyes off the enemy line.

"I got distracted by all the shifters. Sorry," I said and raised my blade by my side.

"There's still time to change your minds and join us," Ealistair shouted.

"No Nightcrawler or witch blood has to be spilled," Rhafnet added.

No response came from our side, and the quiet tension rose between the two factions. There was so much hatred, so much loathing and fear that it brought chills to my spine.

It all came to a breaking point, and I knew things were about to turn ugly.

"Fuck you," Ash shouted, and his voice was like putting an ax through glass, and everyone charged.

The wolves and foxes barreled through us, first growling and howling, while the witches behind Ealistair and Rhafnet attempted to use their powers on the shifters.

Fire, smoke, and blood infiltrated my nose, burning my eyes, wrecking my heart, watching innocent lives sacrifice themselves for nothing. Putting an end to their present and future to defeat or aid a power that shouldn't have been there, and a power that shouldn't even exist.

Yes, the witches that had sided with the demon couple had made a terrible choice, but how many had made it out of real choice, really? The high council was still inactive behind Christian and Hew's possessed bodies. The witches fighting the animals were inexperienced, new to their powers.

Had Ealistair or Christian promised them wealth, power, or a place in society? How did you turn a common man into a pawn for evil?

Foxes, wolves, and witches went down in waves, some losing their lives on the spot, others fighting for survival before being shredded by canines or clawed to death.

A cawing echoed across the bridge as the ravens took flight and attacked those witches that had survived, diving down with their beaks. The bridge shook on their impact with the witches.

That was our cue to go. We broke into a run to get to the other side just as the high council witches also took this as their signal.

I spotted Matilda among the others, the fire bitch that had dared put the responsibility on Caleb for what was going on, and then the moment she'd found out who was behind it had turned her back on everyone else.

She conjured flames from her hand and shot them at all of us, in all directions. I cut through the flames like it was a piece of piñata that erupted on impact.

Caleb ducked away to avoid another one, but Graham caught a flurry of fire and went down. Not for long. A sparkle of dust covered him, and the fires disappeared.

I offered him my hand, and he glared at me for a moment before taking it and helping himself off the ground.

I heard it when I felt it. A sizzle of electricity struck my back, and I braced for the pain. But no pain came.

I opened my eyes, not realizing I'd shut them, and tried to get a look at my back.

"Are you okay?" Caleb asked.

"I-I think so. What happ—" I started to say when I noticed another bolt charging through the air aimed right at Caleb.

Before I knew what I was doing, I pushed him to the side and took the shot, expecting to fall this time.

"See? She was right, Wade," Caleb exclaimed.

I watched my stomach, but there was nothing there, even though there should have been. A charred shirt if nothing else. But no. It was unscathed.

I turned my attention to Caleb, who got off the floor and grinned.

"What do you mean? Who was right?" I asked.

Caleb blinked and shook his head. "Well, they both were actually. Mother Red Cap and Avalis."

"Right about what?"

He placed his hand on my heart, and for a moment my vision blurred, and I felt as if my soul had jumped out of my body and inside Caleb's because I saw myself getting hit by lightning bolts, twice, and coming out unharmed. The moment the charge came anywhere near me, it fizzled into nothingness.

You're a witch, a voice said inside my head, but I couldn't determine if it was Caleb who spoke.

"I am not a witch," I said as soon as Caleb removed his hand from my chest, breaking an empathic connection we'd never experienced before.

"Oh yeah?" he asked, and before I knew it, he'd pushed me into the line of fire. Of literal fire. By Matilda.

The flames shot through the air, but the minute they came within an inch of me, they sizzled out into smoke.

What on earth was going on? Why couldn't I get hurt? Was someone playing tricks on me? This wasn't possible. I would know if someone was playing tricks on me.

"You are a witch. You have been all along. The surge of the ley lines ignited your power. That's why you've been having those outbursts. It wasn't because the spells you'd used were malfunctioning or going haywire. It was because the witch within you was trying to break free. And it did. When we gave ourselves to each other."

I knew I should have doubted every word and told him he was lying, that he was wrong, that I was not a witch, but the moment he'd said it, it was like a light clicked at the back of my mind, and it made sense.

I was a witch.

I'd always been a witch. I'd been a witch-hunter witch. Not that it mattered anymore. At the moment, it didn't matter if I'd spent my life killing my own tribe. It was all in the past, and all I could look into was the future. A future that was at stake. That's what we were fighting for on this bridge. To save lives. Human, witch, Nightcrawler. To give everyone a future.

"Hey!" I heard in front of us and saw Ash shouting from the ground. A witch was on him, his hands completely hidden by black clouds.

I didn't know what his natural power was, and I wasn't going to wait to find out. I now knew what mine was, and I was going to put it to good use.

"Why don't you pick on someone your own size?" I shouted to the witch as I ran to Ash's aid.

The witch looked up at me and grinned.

"With pleasure," he said, and the clouds in his hands shot right at me. Instead of ducking or running away from it, I charged right at it, breaking it away with a wave of my arms.

When I came up to the witch who was looking at me incredulously, my sword went through him like a toothpick, and when I removed the blade, the clouds in his hands vanished.

I looked down at Ash and he got to his feet with a grunt, which stopped as soon as he stood up straight.

"Thanks," he said. "What the hell did you just do?"

I didn't get to answer him. I heard a scream and turned to look at Caleb going past everyone and charging for Ealistair and Hew.

"No!" I shouted.

SEVENTEEN
CALEB

I saw an opportunity, and I took it. There had to be a way to end this bloodbath once and for all.

Let me handle them, Avalis said.

"I don't want you taking control of me. What if you never give it back?"

I'm not like them. I won't hold you a prisoner inside your own body. But you have to let me take care of them.

Whatever assurances she made, I wasn't buying them. No one was good. No one was that pure that they didn't want something in return for their services.

It was the way the world worked. You wanted to use something, you had to pay the price.

If that's what you think, why did you call me? If you were not willing to pay the price, why go through all this?

Because I was desperate. Because I didn't think this through. But it wasn't too late yet.

I still had a buttload of spells to use against them, and Avalis's power, if she let me channel it.

Those spells won't make a dent, and you know it. And I can't let you use my powers. They will destroy you.

Convenient how that was the case, yet she could still conjure teleportation portals to get us here.

That was nothing compared to what I can do.

I came face-to-face with the two demons that had possessed a friend and an enemy.

"What do you think you can do to us?" Ealistair laughed in my face.

I grabbed for a spell and threw it at him, but before it even turned to dust, it disappeared in a vortex of fire.

"Cute. But not good enough," Rhafnet said.

"Why are you doing this? Why are you willing to destroy so many people? For what? You're already powerful enough. What else do you want?"

The story they'd sold at the high council office was good, but barely the truth. If all they wanted was for witches to take control, they could do it by igniting all the dormant witches, if there were any left since the ley line surge, and then taking over the government and any human unit or service. They didn't have to kill humans to do that.

They want to feed, Avalis told me.

"What kind of stupid question is that? We want our rightful place as this world's gods," Ealistair hissed with Christian's voice, only a little deeper. Scarier.

"This is not your world. And you're not welcome here," I yelled.

"Honey." Ealistair turned to Hew. "Will you please get rid of this pest."

Rhafnet smiled and sauntered towards me. She raised her hand, and just before she reached me, her nails turned to claws.

I stepped back to avoid her, but she jumped at me as if she was weightless and slashed my chest.

The pain shot through my body, and the burn of the cut felt like a heavy weight in my head.

As quick as the pain had erupted, it disappeared. And both Rhafnet and I looked at my chest with bewilderment.

I can't do much more if you don't let me take control, Avalis insisted.

That's good enough. I pushed Rhafnet off me.

She came swinging back, clawing at me again, the caw from her lips making the hairs at the back of my neck rise.

I reached for another spell on my gauntlet.

"Shield," I said just as she was about to make impact, and a blue light buzzed in front of me, but it didn't last.

Rhafnet's claws broke through it and shattered it like glass. Her eyes beaded when she took hold of me, and I felt my fear grow tenfold looking into them.

Let me out. I can stop her. Let me out, Avalis pounded in my chest, throwing a tantrum.

The claws dug through my chest again. I swallowed hard as blood gurgled in my throat. I spat it right in Hew's face, but Rhafnet took pleasure in it. She licked her lips, and it felt like her gaze intensified, as though my blood charged her energy and made her stronger. The burn in my chest became unbearable.

Of course she's becoming stronger. She's the mistress of death. Brother, let me handle her, Avalis insisted.

"Get off him, you bitch," I heard someone say, and Rhafnet flew across the space back to Ealistair, and I sat upon the ground.

Mother Red Cap was standing in front of me with a staff in her hand that spread out like fingers in the top, holding a crystal the size of both my hands.

"Mother Red," I called out to her. "What are you doing here? I thought you didn't want to get involved in witch politics." She gave me her hand to help me stand back on my feet.

Her lips pursed.

"Well...I changed my mind. Besides, this isn't witch politics. This is war. And in war, you always take a side." Before I could thank her or say anything to her, she spun on her heel and struck down Rhafnet's effort at attacking her.

"Did you invoke Avalis?" she asked.

I nodded.

"Then where is she?"

Exactly my point, Avalis said.

I pointed at my head in response.

"Why won't you let her out, my dear boy? She's here to help, isn't she?" Mother Red Cap said.

"I-I don't want to lose control of myself. What if she never gives it back, Mother Red Cap?"

"Caleb, don't forget she's the one who destroyed her parents and trapped them under the ley lines in the first place. She's here to help. Not to destroy."

Damn right, I am here to help.

"Also, you can call me Kathleen," she said.

I smiled at her. She had finally trusted us with her real name. And not only that, but she'd chosen to come out of hiding, risking her survival, to help us. Help me.

"Thank you, Kathleen."

She blasted Rhafnet one more time and then turned around and I saw blood in her eyes.

"I can't do this for much longer," she said. "I'm not strong enough to fight a demon. We need Avalis."

Let me help, Caleb. Please.

Ealistair, who had taken an interest in Mother Red Cap, approached us, and he shot fire at her. Kathleen managed to put out the fires, but at the cost of her crystal cracking.

One more flame at her and the crystal turned to dust. Rhafnet pushed Kathleen down and her claws dug into her chest. Hew's body let out an inhumane cry as Rhafnet fed off Mother Red Cap.

She's killing her. Do you want your friend to die? Let me help.

No, I didn't want Mother Red Cap to die. I didn't want anyone else to die. We'd lost enough people already.

Fine, I said, and I felt my consciousness falling over clouds, only there was no gravity. Only suspension in mid-air. And Avalis's power coursed through my body, making me tense with more magic than I'd ever felt in my life.

"*Finally,*" she said.

Rhafnet looked up, and so did Ealistair. If I didn't know any better, I'd have said they were scared, but I knew better, and so did Avalis.

"Who are you?" Ealistair asked, the flames scorching in a circle around him and Rhafnet.

"*Father? You don't recognize your own daughter? I am disappointed.*"

"Avalis?" Rhafnet muttered, her voice breaking before she could fully pronounce her child's name.

"*In the flesh,*" Avalis replied and did a little curtsy for her demon parents as if this was a normal family reunion. "*I heard you're causing humans trouble. I thought I taught you better.*"

Ealistair's eyes narrowed and the flames protecting him and his wife extinguished, leaving him bare in front of the daughter that had once destroyed him.

"This world no longer concerns you, Avalis. You have no business here," he said.

Avalis laughed, and she walked closer to her parents.

"*I could say the same about you. I thought sending you to hell would keep you from harming anyone else, but I guess I'll need to do a better job next time.*"

"Do not defy your father, or this time I won't hesitate ending you," Ealistair shouted, and spit sprayed out of his mouth, his face turning a bright, fiery red.

"*I'll give you one chance to end this nonsense and go back to hell. If you don't, I'll have to do it myself. Again.*" A chill ran through me.

Was Avalis so strong she had the power to do this?

Yes. Yes, she did. I didn't even need to question that. I could feel her unimaginable power coursing through me like a glass jar trying to contain a storm.

Ealistair smirked and took his wife's hand.

"This time we're not afraid to do what's right, Avalis. You can try your best," he said.

Avalis didn't show weakness at his words, but I felt a flash of worry in her that she immediately brushed off. She knew her parents uniting against her could be a task, a task she'd handled once before. But last time they'd held back. And so had she. She had chosen not to destroy them, and they had chosen not to destroy her. It hadn't been a win for either of them, like in the book we'd read. It had been a draw. It had only been a win for humanity.

"*Fine,*" she said and walked closer to her parents.

Ealistair didn't hesitate. He sent a hail of fire in her direction. Avalis raised my hands to stop them, but the energy zapped out of us and we were sent tumbling back, me taking the physical toll and both of us the emotional one.

"*What the...*" she muttered, but once she got us back to our feet she hummed.

What are you doing? she asked me.

I'm not doing anything.

I could feel her confusion and anger building up to something ugly.

Why aren't you letting me use your empathic shield? she asked, and I was immediately lost.

What empathic shield? What did I have to do with stopping her power?

You do know how to use your empathic shield, right? she asked. *Please tell me you know.*

I felt like shaking my head, but I didn't have use of my body. The message was still received by Avalis.

You're an empath, brother, yet no one has shown you the full spectrum of your power. Why?

I had no idea what she was talking about, and I made sure to tell her.

My high priest told me empaths are rare. He's taught me everything he knows.

Then your high priest knows nothing. Let me show you what you're capable of.

I saw Wade make an attempt to step closer, but Avalis raised her hand to tell him to stop. The battle behind us was still going, but I didn't know how long our side would last.

I froze. Everything around us froze. And as soon as

the world stopped moving, I started falling. I fell through the bridge, into the water, past the riverbed, and the cosmos, and the stars, and the universe, until I stood on top of the world with a beautiful woman in front of me.

Her glimmering black skin matched the night sky behind her in beauty, and her hair was made of knots, plaits, and things that couldn't be hair, or from this world.

"Avalis," I said.

She smiled.

"Where...where are we?" I asked and looked around me.

"We're still on the Tower Bridge. Your body is still there. It's just us that are not there."

I frowned.

"What do you mean? We need to go back. They're going to kill everyone if we don't help them. We've got to go back," I said and stepped forward, but I didn't seem to move.

"I can't help them if you don't have full access to your powers, brother. You're an empath, like me. We're linked. That's why you were able to invoke me. And because we're linked, I can't use my powers if you don't know how to use yours."

I took a deep breath, but yet again, it didn't seem like any air came in or went out. We really weren't anywhere real, were we?

"But, by the time you teach me, it will be too late."

Avalis approached me and shook her head.

"Time doesn't exist here. We're in your mind and mine. Time is not a dimension here."

Okay. I tried to make sense of that, but I couldn't get my head around it. How was this possible? How was any of it possible?

"How do we do this?"

Avalis took my hands in hers in response.

"We start by letting me show you what we're capable of," she whispered, and within seconds, I was flooded with emotions. Feelings. Images. Thoughts. Not of Avalis. But of people she'd met. Of people that had come and gone before me. Of times that were solidly in the past.

It all rushed by like a film on fast forward. There was no time to sort through everything that was happening, only to watch, listen, and notice.

"We're connected to the universe, brother. We can speak its language. One touch, and everything is within our reach." I could barely focus on her words when everything around me was a storm of information.

"We can use that. You can use that. You can turn it, twist it, bend it to your will."

She didn't make sense, but at the same time, I understood everything she was talking about. Her power crawled under my skin and made me feel a different person. A new person. A strong person.

"We're the history of the world. We're the emotional history of everything."

Again, everything started falling into place, and I knew what she meant. I knew what we had to do to stop the demons that threatened to destroy that history.

"Now you know," she whispered, and when I opened my eyes, I was back at Tower Bridge with Avalis within me, in control, and the demons closing in on me. On us.

Rhafnet's eyes glowed with the darkness of the night and fear made my skin shiver. I couldn't resist looking into them even though Avalis tried to ward her off us.

Wade stepped between us and Rhafnet, and immediately her deathly touch withered.

We looked at Wade, and he held his body in front of us, using his dampening shield to stop Rhafnet.

He wasn't going to last. He wasn't strong enough. Not like me. Not like us. Avalis forced herself off the ground and touched Wade's shoulder with my hand.

Wade turned his head and looked at me with a strained face. He gritted his teeth as he took the brunt of Rhafnet's wrath.

"*Rest now, brother,*" Avalis told him. "*You've done your part.*"

Wade shook and refused to step aside.

Wade, let go. We've got this, I whispered in his mind, and only then did he stop.

He fell backward to the ground, but I didn't have to worry about him. To check on him. I couldn't even if I wanted to. Avalis was in full fight mode now.

Rhafnet smiled and turned into a giant raven who dove into us and tried to claw at our skin.

"Give up, daughter. This is our kingdom now. And you have lost your place in it," she said, her voice carrying through the air even in her animal form.

Avalis didn't respond. Instead, she reached out her hand and grabbed her mother's claw.

I screamed inside my head, but Avalis knew what she was doing. Rhafnet couldn't hurt us now. She used all her mother's anger and blasted it back at her. Rhafnet flew out across the bridge.

"You ungrateful little shit," Ealistair said, and he sent his flames roaring straight at us.

But Avalis wasn't scared, despite me. And even though I knew what we were capable of, the uncertainty in my head still made me cringe at the impact.

My hand launched, palm outwards, against the fire. When it touched my skin, it didn't burn. Instead, it felt as if we were holding Ealistair and all his hatred.

I could feel his fear and frustration. I could detect his admiration for the daughter he and Rhafnet had birthed, but also the anger that she was getting in the way.

We sent the fire back at him. Just like forcing another's emotions back on them, we forced his power onto him.

He growled and screamed and wailed as his own servant, his own flames, attacked him.

Rhafnet didn't stay down for long. Seeing her husband in danger, she flew back and stepped between us and Ealistair, her eyes emanating the darkness of death that she wanted to inflict on her own child.

But Avalis was done playing. She was no longer giving them a chance. They'd had it and had destroyed a world with it.

Just like Ealistair, Rhafnet's feelings hit us to the core. Her womanhood, her regret, her sorrow. Her motherly instinct turned killer. Her love for her child and her husband. Her hatred for the human race. For what Avalis had done to her other children, the witches. It all felt so clear like it was written as a confession on a piece of paper.

Avalis wasn't taking it. She inflicted it all on her mother. Rhafnet was done killing. She could stop feeding on the death of innocent people. The witches might have been her mother's and her father's creation, but Avalis had made us the way we were meant to be. To keep the world in balance. Safe.

Once upon a time, she'd had hoped to release them from hell, once they'd learned their lesson, but it seemed as if millennia were not enough. Nothing would ever be enough.

There was only one solution. They needed to die. And with it, everything they stood for.

"Avalis, no!" Ealistair said.

"Daughter, don't do this. We're your parents," Rhafnet screamed. "Don't do this to your mother."

Avalis didn't use my mouth to speak. She spoke in their heads. And she didn't need to say much.

Thank you for everything you taught me. Goodbye, she told them, and I could feel her using all her force, all her might to strike back at them.

Don't hurt my friend. Don't hurt Hew, I begged her.

He will not be harmed, she said before both Christian's and Hew's bodies kneeled to the ground, screeching as two entities came out of them.

Two dark shadows that struggled for freedom. But the shadows turned to dust and smoke, and before I knew it, they were gone.

My knees buckled as Avalis weakened.

I don't have much time, she told me.

I know. Thank you for your help. And for everything you showed me.

Without her, I would never have known where I'd come from. Without her, I'd still believe I was lesser because I was an empath. Now I knew.

There's one last thing I need to do, she said and forced me back on my feet.

Everyone was watching us. The fighting had stopped. The high council witches and the ones Ealistair had ignited—because now I knew I hadn't caused the ignition of all the witches in London, but it had all been part of Ealistair's plan—were standing still and watching the demise of their leaders.

The foxes, the wolves, the ravens, the Blades, and the witches on our side were standing next to them looking at me.

"*Brothers and sisters,*" Avalis said through me. "*Witches who betrayed your kind and your duty to this world. You don't deserve your gifts.*"

Avalis raised her hand and formed her fingers into a fist.

"*As punishment for taking my parents' side, your powers will be no more. I take them away from you, just like my parents blessed you with them.*"

The magic crackled in the air and the witches that had taken the wrong side screamed as Avalis removed their magic from them and destroyed it for good.

Avalis's strength was dwindling. She was using more and more of herself to help this world. She'd already given most of her power to take down the demons. Now it was her turn to fall.

"*And to you, Nightcrawlers, witches who took my side, I wish I could give you your lost ones back. But know that your actions will forever change the world. I will take knowledge of your existence from the human world, but the carnage that was caused will still live in their memory.*" As her words weakened, my body was released, the energy of her goddess power inside me bursting into tiny fragments.

And then I was all alone inside my head again.

Eighteen

Wade

Caleb buckled as Avalis released him back to me, and I ran to get him before he completely collapsed. His face looked drained of all blood, and the circles under his eyes were saggy and darker than before, but I didn't care. He'd just carried a goddess inside him and destroyed two other gods. I was super proud of him.

"Easy. Easy," I told him as I put my hands under his arms and steadied him.

I helped him find his footing and put one of his arms over my neck, then grabbed onto his waist with my free hand.

"How are you feeling?" I asked him.

His head barely moved in my direction as he said, "World's worst hangover."

I chuckled. Even at his worst, this man knew how to make me laugh. He never lost his humor. Not even when times were so hard that we didn't know if we'd make it through to the other end unscathed.

Ash came over to him and put Caleb's other hand around him. I swallowed a possessive snarl even though I felt like ripping his head off for touching my man.

Since when did I want to rip men's throats for touching Caleb? Was this the mating bond talking or something else? Something completely different? Something I'd been chasing my whole life?

"Caleb, are you feeling okay?" Ash asked and looked into his eyes.

After everything that had happened between them, I didn't know how he had the audacity to do so. And I didn't know how Caleb must have felt with his bullshit right in his face.

I looked over, behind Ash, to the sea of witches and familiars. The foxes, wolves, and ravens. They all had turned human. The ones who'd survived anyway. I could see more than a few fox bodies still lying on the ground, unmoving, and enough wolves to feel like I was at the vet's morgue. Familiars who'd given their lives to stop the high council and the demons who controlled them. I'd done my best to help them. I'd tried to protect them from as many attacks as possible with my newfound powers, but there was only one of me and so many of them, it hadn't been enough.

The witches had the least amount of casualties, not so surprising, but had more answering to do. Most of the high council stood frozen, looking at Caleb in shock. The newer witches who'd sided with Ealistair and Rhafnet had been apprehended by Lloyd and the rest of the surviving BLADE force.

Winston ran across the bridge over to Hew, breaking the stillness. Graham stepped up to Caleb, and so did Lorelai.

"What have you done?" Graham cried, and I glared at him.

How many times did we have to fight the things he and his high council had caused? How many more excuses would he find for what they'd done? He'd taken our side this time, but was he really good?

"I did what I had to do. Avalis did the rest," Caleb croaked.

He still didn't sound like the Caleb I knew, but he'd get there. All he needed was a good cup of Annabel's tea, and he'd be back to the Caleb I loved in no time.

Loved. The word came so easily now when it was only a dream before I met him. I'd been fooled for so many years, denied my first crushes, relationships, everything normal, and even after everything that had gone down with Christian and finding out the truth, I still didn't know what normal was.

That moment, with Caleb pinned next to me, weak and powerless, I knew one thing. I might never know if I'd truly loved Sarah and if Christian had manipulated my sexuality and emotions more than I was aware of, but if there was one thing I was certain of, it was that I loved Caleb.

"What happened here today?" a wolfman asked.

I hadn't seen him before, but by the way the others looked at him, I would have said he was their leader.

"Two demons tried to decimate everyone—" I started.

"And with the help of another we killed them off," Caleb added.

The wolfman didn't look too happy with the response.

"We only came as a favor to Lorelai. And instead, I got half my pack dead or wounded. How are the witches planning on making this up to the wolves?"

"And the foxes," Lorelai added.

Everyone turned to Graham, Ash, and the few of the high council members with any power left.

Graham struggled to get any words out, and Ash looked around him at the bloodbath, surely looking for an appropriate response.

"The coven needs some re-organization," someone said behind me, and when I turned, I saw Mother Red Cap talking, taking small steps towards the wolf. "I'm sure once they've figured out the punishment fitting to the traitors, they will lend a helping hand to the Nightcrawlers."

"Isn't losing our powers punishment enough?" Matilda screeched from behind the wolfman.

Everyone glared at her.

"Not even close," Ash said.

I was glad to see he hadn't completely lost his confidence.

"Mother Red," the wolf said. "I didn't think you dealt with the witches anymore."

All eyes turned to her, and her gaze narrowed. How did he know her? He had called her by her name while the witches weren't familiar with her or her power. Did she make herself known to those she chose? Or had they found her by chance?

"I don't. And I still won't. I will keep helping my children of the night. Let that not be a concern or fear," Mother Red Cap replied.

Children of the night? Was she known to the Nightcrawlers? Was she helping them behind the high council's back? Surely they would have found out about her if she had a name in the Nightcrawler world.

"So you *are* real!" Graham said and stared at her. "All the rumors and the speculations."

"Yes, you finally meet me, Graham. After trying so hard for years," Mother Red Cap answered him then turned to the wolf. "Come, Nolan, let me help those that are still breathing." She gave the wolfman her hand, and he took it and kissed it before leading her down to the first wolf who was bleeding.

"So much destruction," Caleb murmured, and I turned to him.

"I know," I said and squeezed his hand. "I tried to stop them, but—"

"It's not your fault."

"It's not yours, either."

He closed his eyes, and I thought I'd have to drill it into his head, but I was surprised with what he said next.

"I know it's not. I know now. But whatever happens next is going to be."

"What do you mean?" I asked.

I didn't know how the aftermath would be his fault when the war itself hadn't been.

"I'm the face of this destruction. Did you hear Avalis? Everything is going to change. She tried to show me, but she didn't make it long enough. Whatever happens next, it's not going to be easy," he said, and he opened his eyes to look back at the scene on the bridge.

"You're forgetting something, mate," I said and squeezed his hand again. "You're not alone in this."

I wanted to tell him I loved him, but something stopped me from saying it aloud. I didn't know if I needed to anyway. I was sure my emotions were so overwhelming that he got the message.

"I was scared there for a second," I told him. "I thought I was going to lose you. Again."

"No, never again." He smirked.

Lorelai came closer and brushed some of Caleb's hair off his face.

"Are you all right? Next time I see you, you gotta tell me what happened here," she said, and I could see more than curiosity in her eyes. "I'll try and save face as much as possible, but...no guarantees."

She looked over to Graham.

"What's happening with the high council? Are you going to step up?"

"No," Caleb said. "Things need to change."

"I don't know, sweetheart," Graham said, completely ignoring Caleb. "Ash and the others will have a meeting and discuss how we move on from this."

"Keep me in the loop, yeah? I got to go," Lorelai said, and she retreated with the rest of the foxes to help them clear the bodies of those who'd fallen.

"So, Mr. Rawthorne." Graham addressed me before I could talk to Lloyd who was approaching us. "You're a witch after all."

Coming from him, it felt like an insult when it should have felt like a badge of honor. Yes, I knew the irony of being made to kill my own kind. I wasn't stupid. It didn't mean it gave Graham any right to judge me.

"I guess I am," I said, matching his tone, challenging him to say or do anything stupid.

Instead of doing any of that, he smirked.

"Now that we know, I can teach you," he offered.

Before I even got a chance to tell him I'd rather be fucked by a tree and have my cock blown by a rose bush, Caleb said something simpler, but with far more authority than my insult would have achieved.

"Not a bloody chance."

"Wade, the guys are helping out the wounded familiars, but is there anything you want me to do?" Lloyd asked, seemingly ignoring the new part of my identity.

I looked behind him at the small group of hunters that were offering water or medical assistance to the wolves that had turned back to human form despite their lacerations and bruises.

It shouldn't have been just them out there doing what was needed. I wanted to be among them. It was the least I could do. But I couldn't leave Caleb alone. Not when I had almost lost him too.

"Help the humans out of their cars and into safety," I said. "Help anyone you can. I need to make sure Caleb is okay and then I'll join you."

Lloyd nodded and left, and I took Caleb to the edge of the bridge so he could sit with his back against the side. I spotted Winston in the middle with a weak, but very much alive, Hew in his arms, next to Christian's dead body. Or at least, I hoped it was dead. I couldn't even begin to imagine having to fight that asshole again. Not now. Not ever.

"Do you have a spell that can help?" I asked, bringing my attention back to Caleb.

He fiddled with his gauntlets and handed me a green stone.

"This," he said.

"Why are you giving it to me?"

"I'm too weak to cast anything. You can help, though."

I knew what he was implying, but I didn't know if I was ready. I barely knew how to use my natural power, how on earth was I supposed to cast a spell?

I shook my head in response, but Caleb wasn't having it. He squeezed my fist around the spell and looked me in the eyes.

"You can do this. I can walk you through it."

I wanted to protest and tell him there were dozens more witches more qualified than me to do this, but a part of me was intrigued by all of this.

"Close your eyes," he ordered, and the command with the mix of the spell in my hand was enough to wake little Wade in my pants.

So not the right time, dude. So not the right time.

"Now let the energy of the spell flow through you. It's like a pulse. The stone should feel like a heartbeat. Feel it. Hear it. Let it match yours," Caleb whispered close to my ear.

I concentrated on the heat in my hand. The heat made by my tightening fist. Or so I thought. The heat didn't just pulse, it felt radiant. As if I was holding the sun in my hand and I was about to burn. The energy traveled up my arm, giving me goosebumps, and down to my groin, only making my cock harder and my knees weaker.

All of a sudden, I felt a rhythm in my ear. I couldn't hear it, but it felt like a throbbing on my drums. A throbbing that pounded against me until it was the only thing I could concentrate on.

"Good. Very good. Now say '*cura*.'" Caleb's breath on my ear was the only reason why I heard what he said.

I thought it before I spoke it, and when my mouth uttered the words, it felt as if I'd opened a secret door to the end of the universe. The coolness chilled my body like a bucket of ice water that washed off me, and I felt it pushing through my hands onto Caleb.

When I opened my eyes, it was just in the nick of time to see the dust settling on his skin before it got absorbed into his pores. In an instant, the color returned to his face, and his eyes looked more vibrant than ever.

"You did it!" he said and hugged me.

I had done it. I'd performed my first, official spell. I was a witch after all. But, what did that mean about me? About my family. About my mom. About my dad...

"Don't worry," Caleb said. "We'll figure it out."

"I know."

Together, I added, not sure if he could hear it.

Together, he said back.

I had truly healed him. It was impossible to believe. I was a witch and I'd healed my boyfriend.

"Let's go home," Caleb said, and I couldn't agree more.

It was time to go home to our little tribe.

———

Demon Heart has come to a finish, but Wade's and Caleb's adventures continue in Vampire Heart.

What's next for the couple? How will Wade deal with his new-found witch identity? What will happen with the High Council? And is Christian really dead?

Find out in Vampire Heart, Book 3 of the Cursed Hearts series!

A Letter from Rhys

I hope you enjoyed Demon Heart and the continuing adventures of Wade, Caleb, and their crew.

A review is always appreciated. If you think you can take 2 minutes of your time to post your opinion on Amazon it would go a long way towards earning you good karma points and meeting your familiar mate. For reals!

Demon Heart is probably my favorite book I have written to-date. I wasn't sure, initially, if I wanted to go this big on the second installment, but considering most series or trilogies suffer in the second book, I knew I had nothing to lose. I'm aware a lot of you are curious about the mythology behind many of the Nightcrawler species or the BLADE force, but I have purposefully kept certain things off the page because there's so much that I didn't want to bore you with. I also didn't want to write myself into a corner creatively so I could have more freedom to do other series or standalones set in the same world.

I had a lot of "surprise" characters pop up on the pages during the writing process of this book as well that have inspired me. I'm not going to tell you my favorite side characters, but if you want to see a certain character's story on page, you can email me, message me, or shout it from the rooftops, and your wish may just come true.

But before I delve into other books, it's time for Caleb and Wade to face more enemies and have a pickle or two to get out of.

Demon Heart was probably the easiest book to write in the series, or possibly ever, I think, partly because I had an almost clear vision of what I wanted to happen after Killer Heart, and mainly because once I had the plot down, I didn't have the time to worry if it was good enough or not. I just had to write it.

Let me explain.

Sometimes, I will book all my slots with my editor in one go. Victoria, my wonderful creature who perseveres through all my rough manuscripts and manages to come out unscathed, is a busy woman, so if I want to use her, I need to book her in advance.

I find doing that also helps give me a deadline to finish the book and work backwards from that.

Well, guess what happened?

Killer Heart took longer to edit because it was mainly dictated and mixed in with life (why do I never account for life's distractions?) and I ended up with two weeks to spare before the completed manuscript had to be in her hands.

So what did I do?

Booked myself away for four days in a remote hotel so I could get some serious progress made. I finished pretty much the entire book in those four days. Writing it from dawn to dusk, in my hotel room, at breakfast, at the bar, in the lobby, then back in the room.

It was a great experience, although rather exhausting, as you can imagine. If I learned one thing from it, it's that I can write fast and my creativity is not restricted by stress or pressure. Isn't that great?

I will admit I almost had a nervous breakdown with the number of deadlines and responsibilities, and for that reason, I did have to push the editing slot for book 3 back by a couple of months.

While I could write every day and not give a damn about anything else, the pressure of everything that surrounds both a day job and publishing can become too much. So another valuable lesson learned. Don't push myself over my limits.

I'm glad I re-scheduled my editing slot and have given myself some breathing room because it allowed me to put some distance between the works (and do lots of admin), which gave me a better perspective over the direction of the series.

So make sure to check out Vampire Heart, the next book in the series.

If you want to get more and frequent updates about what I'm up to, then make sure to join my Facebook group **Rhys Everly After**.

https://www.facebook.com/groups/everlyafter/

If you're not a social media kind of person, then you can always sign up to my newsletter (which goes out weekly) and this is where I make all my big announcements. Don't forget, you also get the free short set in the Cursed Hearts universe, Cursed Mate, when you do.

I can't wait to hear what you thought of Demon Heart.

See you in the next book.

Rhys Lawless
December 2019

Audiobooks

My books are coming in audio. For an up-to-date list visit my website at rhyswritesromance.com/audio

Rhys Lawless

Killer romance. One spell at a time.

Cursed Hearts Series:

Narrated by John York

Killer Heart, Book 1

Roman & Jude Series:

Narrated by John York

Elven Duty, Book 1

Elven Game, Book 2

Elven Heir, Book 3

———

Rhys Everly

Sexy romance with all the feels

A Proper Education Series

Narrated by John York

Teach for Treat

Beau Pair

Me Three

Your Only Fan

Missing Linc

Cedarwood Beach Series

Narrated by Nick Hudson

Fresh Start, Book 1

About the Author

Rhys Everly-Lawless is a hopeless romantic who loves happily-ever-afters.

Which would explain why he loves writing them.

When he's not passionately typing out his next book, you can find him cuddling his dog, feeding his husband, or taking long walks letting those plot bunnies breed ferociously in his head.

He writes contemporary gay romances as Rhys Everly and LGBTQ+ urban fantasy and paranormal romances as Rhys Lawless.

You can find out more about him and his works-in-progress by joining his Facebook group or visiting his website rhyswritesromance.com

Index

Avalis - Goddess/Demon of Compassion. An empath creature who can only be invoked by an empath witch, by mating with another being in a ritual of blood and sex.

Blade - a witch hunter's sword. Also slang term for a witch hunter.

BLADE force - the task force of witch hunters whose sole purpose is to find and eliminate witches.

Coven - a group of witches, usually based on geographical location.

Crown Jewels - Powerful spells kept in the Tower of London and guarded by the seven raven familiars under the Queen's command.

Cyclops - A Nightcrawler species descended from giants.

Demon - a higher entity with unimaginable power. Term is interchangeable with God/dess.

Dhampir - A very rare Nightcrawler species. Energy vampires.

Dust - The effect of a spell being cast which in turn turns to residue. It fades off after a certain time, depending on the strength of the spell.

Ealistair - God/Demon of War. Has been trapped under the ley lines for thousands of years. Can be invoked by sacrificing 5 powerful witches at key points of magical convergence in London.

Empathy - the ability to feel the emotions of others.

Familiar - a shifter. Protectors of witches. They bond and mate for life with witches who they are destined to protect.

Green Mile - A pub where humans aware of the paranormal world meet and mingle with Nightcrawlers.

High Council - the governing body of a coven.

High Priest/ess - a member of the high council.

Ignition - The process of awakening a witch's powers, including their natural power and their spell casting abilities.

Incubus - A Nightcrawler species that feeds off sex. If you get an Incubus to fall for you, then you've found a partner for life. Plus, great sex forever. A female incubus is called succubus.

Lacing - the process of mixing energy with a physical object.

Mated App - An app for Nightcrawlers. Primarily used for familiars to find their mates, but also used for hook-ups.

Natural power - a witch's inherent power that does not require the use of a spell.

Nightcrawler - Paranormal creatures.

Phoenix - a rare and immortal Nightcrawler species that regenerates from their own ashes. They can also heal others by sacrificing part or all of themselves.

Potion - Lesser common use of magic. Usually in liquid form.

Rhafnet - Goddess/Demon of Death. She has been trapped under the ley lines with her husband after her daughter, Avalis, put her there. Can only be invoked by a psychic witch.

Spell - a crystal of various sizes and colours created by alchemy that can be used by witches to perform magical tasks. A spell can be cast by a word or phrase called a spellword.

Spellword - a word or phrase that casts a spell.

The Crow - Nightcrawler and Witch pub.

Tower of London - Primarily a safe place for powerful spells. Secondarily, a ley line intersection.

Troll - Earth Nightcrawlers with immense strength. They are a secretive species and not much is known about them other than they are the strongest species of Nightcrawlers.

Vampire - A Nightcrawler species that feeds off blood.

Xtasy - supernatural and human club in Soho, frequented by a primarily queer population.

Made in the USA
Middletown, DE
13 March 2023

26713782R00163